Oops! I Summoned a Night Demon

Witches Love Monsters

Tiffany Roberts

Oops! I Summoned a Night Demon

When she wished upon a star, she never thought the universe would manifest him.

Ember has always worked hard to achieve her goals. Move to the city? Check. Start her own boutique? Check. Buy a Victorian house? Check. Find love?

Absolute failure, and it's not for lack of trying.

So she does something she hasn't tried yet—she makes a wish upon a star. It's just a silly, hopeful gesture. What can it hurt?

With a literal bump in the night, Nyte appears. He's ethereally gorgeous, with dark skin that glitters like the starry sky, wings formed of otherworldly shadow, and eyes that glow with all the beauty, depth, and mystery of the universe. The moment Ember sees him, she can't help but think her wish has come true.

What does it matter that he's not human? He's her monster-loving fantasy brought to life.

The problem? He's still heartbroken over his freaking ex.

Thanks to the spell that inadvertently summoned him, she

has a month to prove that she's the one for him. That she's worthy of his love.

But is his wounded heart able to give it?

Check the author's website for content warnings.

Copyright © 2025 by Tiffany Freund and Robert Freund Jr.

All Rights Reserved. No part of this publication may be used or reproduced, distributed, or transmitted in any form by any means, including scanning, photocopying, uploading, and distribution of this book via any other electronic means without the permission of the author and is illegal, except in the case of brief quotations embodied in critical reviews and certain other noncommercial uses permitted by copyright law. For permission requests, contact the publishers at the address below.

Tiffany Roberts

authortiffanyroberts@gmail.com

This book was not created with AI, and we do not give permission for our work to be trained for AI.

This book is a work of fiction. Names, characters, places, and incidents are products of the author's imagination or are used fictitiously and are not to be construed as real. Any resemblance to actual events, locales, organizations, or people, living or dead, is entirely coincidental.

Cover and Character Illustration by Morgan Lee

To everyone who's ever wished upon a star and didn't get a two-dicked demon...
We got you.

And to Regine Abel, Opal Reyne, and Naomi Lucas—we love you!

Chapter One

The streets of Salem, Massachusetts were bustling as Ember approached the Broomstick Tavern. She was used to this sort of activity. It came with living in a tourist city, and while she knew some locals didn't care for it, she loved it. She loved the culture, loved the vibes, loved how lively it was. It was why she'd moved here nearly ten years ago.

Well, that and because Ember adored anything and everything to do with horror, the supernatural, and goth fashion. It was also the perfect location for her boutique.

Between this town, her shop, and finally buying her dream house, everything was going great in her life.

Except when it came to dating.

But that wasn't stopping her from trying. Tonight, she was on her way to meet a guy she'd recently matched with on an online dating app.

God, am I really doing this again?

You never know, Ember. Maybe this will be it. Maybe he's the one.

Who could say? Trent was cute, and based on her conversations with him thus far, he seemed like a good guy—with *seemed* being the key word there. Though Ember had gone through this routine a few times already, she'd yet to have any luck.

She was thirty-two years old and still single. But it wasn't like she was going to find someone unless she tried.

If true love is going to happen to me, it's sure taking its sweet time.

Her boot heels tapped on the sidewalk, and the September breeze caressed her legs, which were on display thanks to her green satin and lace open-front skirt. Reaching the tavern, Ember came to a stop near the door and took a moment to pull out her phone, turn on the camera, and give herself a once-over. Her makeup still looked good, so she tucked her loose hair behind her ears before shooting Trent a text.

Me: I'm here!

Trent: already got a spot inside

Ember smiled. He wasn't late and had already secured a table. Those were marks in his favor.

Taking hold of the handle, she pulled the door open and stepped inside. She walked into a cacophony created by overlapping conversations, laughter, and the sounds of people eating and drinking. The establishment was dark, illuminated by the orange glow of black lanterns hanging from the ceiling and walls and perched upon the tables. The brightest light came from the big screen TVs mounted behind the bar. Large straw brooms and framed art of witches decorated the walls.

As she scanned the tables, her brow furrowed. Trent was

nowhere to be seen. Did she have the right place? She was sure he'd told her to meet him here.

"Amber!"

Ember turned her head toward the shout to find Trent sitting on a stool at the bar, grinning. His short blonde hair was slicked back, and he wore blue jeans and a white baseball jersey with red trim.

Wait, did he just call me Amber?

And why was he sitting at the bar? Hadn't he said he—

He said he had a spot inside. Not a table.

Okay, that's not a huge deal. The bar is fine. As for my name...

It wasn't like he'd misheard her. Her name was written plainly on her dating profile. Maybe she'd misheard him over the noise?

He waved, and as though they weren't making direct eye contact, called, "Over here, Amber!"

Nope. I heard him right.

Letting out a calming breath, she made her way toward the bar, weaving through the tables and patrons.

Trent slipped off his stool as she neared, and his brown eyes dipped, taking her in. He didn't bother hiding the lust in his eyes. "Wow, you're hotter than in your picture."

Ember inwardly cringed. Definitely not off to a good start. She smiled and gestured at him. "And you...look like you!"

He smirked, running a hand over his hair in an obvious attempt to show off his muscled bicep. "Pretty good looking myself, huh?"

She pointed to the stool next to the one he'd vacated. "Is that mine?"

Trent glanced back. "Oh, yeah. Sit down." He dropped back onto his seat and motioned to the mugs on the counter. "I already ordered us beers."

Ember pulled out the stool and sat, tugging down the short front of her skirt to keep her thighs covered before setting her purse on the bar top. "Thanks, but I'm not a fan of beer."

"Oh, come on." He slid the mug toward her. "It's good stuff. At least try a few sips. It won't hurt you."

"I'd rather not. I find beer gross."

"Uh oh, red flag, am I right?" Trent laughed much too enthusiastically at his own joke and nudged her with his arm. "Just kidding. More for me!"

She smiled tightly and pushed the mug toward him. "Have at it."

He turned on his stool so he was facing her, once again ogling her. "What are you, some kind of earth witch or something with all the green?"

His gaze lingered on her breasts, where the neckline of her off-shoulder blouse dipped in a V. And considering she was full-chested and wearing a pushup bra, she was sure he was getting an eyeful.

I wish I was a witch. Then maybe I'd have a spell to get out of this.

"Not a witch," she said, pulling up the neckline a bit, hoping he'd get the hint. "I just like to dress up."

"Isn't that a bit childish?" He picked up one of the beers and drank.

And there it is.

She pressed her lips together. How was she not surprised by his response? "What's childish about it?"

Trent shrugged and lowered the mug, licking the foam from his upper lip. "I don't know. Just a thing kids do, isn't it? Playing dress-up. Anyway, you looked goth in your profile picture. Guess I was expecting you to be decked out in black, is all."

"Some days I am."

The bartender stepped in front of Ember. "Can I get you anything?"

Ember smiled politely at him. "Water, please."

The man nodded and filled up a glass, setting it in front of her. "Anything to eat?"

"Get me a double cheeseburger and fries with a side of garlic wings," Trent said.

Nodding, the bartender looked at Ember. "And you?"

"Just a basket of fries, please."

As soon as the bartender was gone, Trent rested his arm on the bar and leaned close, his lips stretching into a sly smile. "So, Amber, I've really been looking forward to—"

"It's Ember."

"Huh? Oh, shit. Really? I thought it was Amber this whole time." He laughed and shook his head. "Anyway, I've been looking forward to meeting you. I like to see the person I'm talking to. Texting ain't the same, you know?"

Ember picked up her glass of water and took a sip. "Mmhmm."

He stared at her mouth. "You know, you really are beautiful…"

"So what do you like to do for fun?"

"Hang out with the boys, throw back a few, catch a game. Doesn't take much to make me happy."

"You said you worked at a home repair company?"

"Yeah. Sales department, so you know what that means."

"Uh, don't think I do."

Smirking, Trent took a long swig of his beer, then wiped his lips with the back of his hand. "Big commissions. I upsell the shit out of everything we have. Pulling in six figures."

"Good for you. It's great to be passionate about your work."

He grunted. "It's work, and I like money. Oh, hey. Didn't you say that you just bought a house?"

"I did. Just moved in a week ago."

"I could drop by and check—"

"No, no, it's okay," Ember hurried to say with a slight wave, definitely not wanting him anywhere near her house.

Trent chuckled. "It doesn't have to be work related. We could get to know each other more...*intimately*." He grazed a finger over the bare skin of her thigh.

Ember jerked her legs away as a shudder coursed through her.

Oh ew, ew, ew, ew.

She rubbed a hand over the spot he'd touched as though she could erase the memory of it. "This isn't going to work."

Brow furrowing, Trent sat up straight. "What?"

"This." She grabbed her purse and slipped off the stool as she drew the strap over her shoulder. "I'm leaving."

"But you just got here."

"And I've seen all I need to."

His face twisted into a scowl as he stood, blocking her from moving away. "What the fuck does that mean?"

Ember glared up at him. "Please step aside."

"Not until you tell me what the hell is going on."

"Please step aside."

"Amber, come o—"

"It's *Ember!*"

"Ma'am, is everything okay?" a man asked from the stool beside Trent.

"Everything is fine," Trent snapped.

"No, everything is not fine. I want to leave," Ember said.

"Tell me why."

She closed her eyes and pinched the bridge of her nose, begging for the patience to keep from hitting him, because she was *this* close to swinging if he didn't move his ass out of the way. And she really didn't want to spend the night in a jail cell for battery.

Of course there was also the more immediate danger of him hitting her back. Trent was larger and stronger than her, and he wasn't showing much restraint when it came to anger and aggression.

Drawing in a deep breath, she opened her eyes and met his gaze. "I don't owe you any explanation, but I'll give you one anyway." She held up a finger. "One, you didn't even know my name. Two, you assumed what I wanted to drink and then expected me to accept it after it was sitting out of my sight for who knows how long. Three, you're rude and insulting. Four, we're not compatible at all. And five, you touched me and tried to invite yourself to my house for sex. Absolutely not."

"Then what the fuck was the point of this?"

Because of course this guy just wanted sex to satisfy his plus-size goth girl fetish.

I fucking hate dating.

"Trent, you're an asshole, and I just dodged a bullet."

"Whatever," he sneered. "You're an ugly fat bitch anyway. I was doing you a favor."

Ember wrinkled her nose at him. "Seriously? Get out of my way."

Trent thrust his hand toward the bar. "You gonna pay for your beer?"

"It's your beer."

Not caring if the police were called at this point, she stepped forward and shouldered past him.

"Bitch!" he yelled over the din.

Ember flipped him off as she made her way to the door, unable to get out of the place fast enough. As soon as the door closed behind her and she was briskly walking away from the tavern, she pulled out her phone, blocked his number, and deleted her profile from the dating app.

I am soooo done with men.

She'd seen plenty of videos on social media of other women telling their nightmare dating stories. Ember had her own share, but this one took the top spot on her worst dates list.

Why couldn't she meet someone decent? Someone who didn't judge her based on her looks or mock her for what she wore? She'd been dealing with it ever since grade school. You'd think that as men grew older they'd mature, at least a little. But nope. Some men remained juvenile pricks their whole lives.

You should stop expecting to find love and romance like in the novels you read, Ember.

Her lips curled into a smirk. The men in her favorite books weren't human, they were otherworldly aliens and supernatural monsters. Big difference.

But unfortunately, they weren't real.

Ember was lonely and tired. Tired of getting her hopes up, tired of searching for something, for someone, that didn't exist.

Except that wasn't true. Her friend Maggie had found a wonderful man who worshipped the ground she walked on. She'd found true love, a Gomez and Morticia type of love.

Why couldn't Ember?

She gazed up at the sky.

Maybe love isn't in the stars for me?

Fifteen minutes later, she reached the path leading to her front door. She stopped and looked at her new home. The green two-story Victorian was a bit of a fixer upper, with a patchy, shingled roof, peeling paint, and a porch with a bit of sag, but it was hers. All her hard work and saving had paid off.

She couldn't help but smile to herself, chest swelling with a sense of accomplishment.

Ember walked to the front door, fishing out her keys. The

porch creaked as she stepped onto it. As soon as she let herself in and locked the door behind her, she removed her boots and made her way through the gloom to the kitchen, where she flicked on the lights and set her purse on the counter. Having missed out on dinner at the tavern, she threw together a turkey and cheese sandwich and ate it while putting away the dishes in the dish rack.

The quiet in the house was deafening, making her all the more aware of how alone she was.

With a sigh, she grabbed her phone, turned off the lights, and took the stairs up to the second floor, entering her bedroom and plugging in her phone to charge on the nightstand.

In the connected bathroom, Ember brushed her teeth and took a quick shower, washing away the scent of the tavern and the disgusting feel of Trent's touch. As minor as it had been, it still had made her skin crawl. Once she'd blow dried her hair, she pulled on a white nightgown and slipped back into her room.

After the noise of the bar, the quiet was preferable, even despite the loneliness that came with it. So she lit a stick of incense and picked up a book to read to unwind before bed. She could lose herself in a fantasy world filled with sexy monsters and forget about the shitty date. She could forget about shitty human men altogether.

But not long after she lay down, the heat in the room grew uncomfortable.

What she wouldn't have given for central air conditioning. But it wasn't in the budget yet, and the coming fall was bringing cooler temperatures. If it would just bring them a little faster, she'd be set.

Sitting up, Ember opened the window next to her day bed, letting in the night air. The breeze brushed over her, and she closed her eyes as it cooled her skin.

She opened her eyes and stared up at the sky. The full moon hung low, dimmed by hazy clouds. The stars weren't bright, they never were here in the city, but she could still make some out.

A bright star streaked across the sky, disappearing behind the clouds.

Ember's breath caught. When was the last time she'd seen a shooting star? As a child?

She chuckled as she folded her arms atop the metal frame of her daybed and leaned out the window. She didn't know what possessed her, didn't know why she was filled with a sudden, whimsical urge to make a wish, but the words came out nonetheless.

"Starlight, starbright," she began, face heating, "first star I see tonight. I... I wish for love. A deep, abiding love. A love that's unwavering, unconditional, that's never judgmental. A love that feels...fated. Please, send me someone who I can forever trust with my heart."

As soon as she'd made her wish...nothing happened.

Well, of course nothing would happen. What did you expect? To feel a rush of magic? To see fireworks go off in the sky and form a giant arrow pointing you right to your fated lover?

With a wistful sigh, Ember dropped back onto her bed, feeling absolutely ridiculous. But she couldn't help the sadness creeping into her heart as she picked up her book.

She lay down and tried to forget she'd made that silly wish. "I guess I can continue dreaming about fictional love..."

And so she read, losing herself in the story, until her eyelids drifted shut and she lost herself in her dreams instead.

Chapter Two

In her sleep, Ember didn't see the same star streak across the sky again. She didn't see it glimmering as it sped toward her house and flitted in through her open window, or she would've known that it wasn't a star at all—for what star was small enough to fit in her hand?

She didn't see the silver light falling across her walls, floor, and bed. And she didn't hear the mischievous, tinkling giggle that echoed through her room.

The light moved closer to the human, hovering above her and casting its glow upon her. "What have we here?"

The human was quite pleasing to look upon. The black roots of her hair faded into long silver strands that shimmered beneath Starling's light, and her skin was pale and smooth. Black, fanned lashes rested over her sharp cheekbones, and thick, dark brows arched above her closed eyes. Her features were bold yet delicate. She could've seduced even an incubus with a sultry curl of her full lips.

Starling's gaze roamed past the human's face to her body, clad in a short white nightgown. The almost sheer material clung to every voluptuous curve, accentuating her generous breasts, soft belly, and flaring hips while leaving her long, thick, shapely legs bare.

The sprite grinned. "Ah, you are perfect for him."

Because it was far more than this woman's beauty calling to Starling. Magic dwelled within this mortal, powerful and brilliant, slumbering in her chest. Untapped but present. And that was all Starling needed.

She giggled again. "Finally. There will be an end to his moping."

Whisking under the bed, the sprite darted about, trailing stardust upon the floor in her wake. Once the summoning circle was complete, she flitted back up and hovered over the human's face.

"Oh, yes. You are *perfect*...but you have much work to do." Starling leaned close and whispered in the human's ear. "Summon him, witchling."

As Starling spoke the words of the incantation, the woman repeated them in her sleep, her voice resonating through the room with an arcane thrum.

The summoning circle blazed with blue-white light, casting deep shadows on the ceiling overhead.

Chapter Three

Violent shaking startled Ember to alert wakefulness. Heart hammering, she jolted upright. The bed trembled, its metal frame rattling.

Oh God, is this an earthquake?

She crawled to the edge of the mattress to seek shelter in a safer location only to freeze when she saw the floor. Blue-white light shone from beneath the bed, covering everything in an ethereal glow that deepened and stretched the shadows in the room. The air was charged, bristling with static electricity, and she felt it buzzing on her skin.

That sensation intensified as the shadows began to bleed into the light, overtaking it on the outskirts of the room and then creeping toward her bed with increasing speed, covering more and more of the space in darkness.

"This is definitely not an earthquake!" she whispered.

Ember's eyes widened, and she scrambled backward, kicking at the covers until her back hit the bed frame.

The light brightened, but it did nothing to fight the expanding darkness. The bed vibrated more forcefully, making her book tumble over the edge and thump on the floor. She grasped the metal bars behind her.

The darkness closed in around her.

Ember whimpered, curling against the bed frame, and squeezed her eyes shut as she ducked her head. There was a roaring in her ears, growing louder, and louder, and louder.

Then it all stopped. The roaring, the rattling, the prickling sensation on her skin.

Tentatively, she opened her eyes and lifted her head. Both the unnatural blackness and the bright light were gone, leaving her room in perfectly normal nighttime darkness.

Ember ran a hand through her hair, sweeping it back. "What the fuck was that?"

A sudden bang beneath her bed wrenched a cry from her, and she almost didn't hear the muttered curse from below over the sound of her own voice.

There was a scratch on the hardwood floor, followed by a rasping sound as though something was sliding out from beneath her bed.

"Of all the impractical, undignified places to draw a summoning circle..."

Ember's breath hitched, and her eyes flared. That was a voice. A voice! A deep, velvety, masculine voice with a hint of a growl that seeped into her, warming her from within. No voice should've sounded that alluring, that otherworldly, especially if it belonged to...to what? The monster under her bed?

A figure emerged from the darkness. Its shape was humanoid, but it seemed to be comprised of shadows blacker than the blackest night. As it shifted, a pair of eyes settled on Ember, gleaming like twin stars in the otherwise lightless void of space. Wings of shadow unfurled behind the figure.

More glittering stars blinked into existence across the creature, turning it into a tapestry of the night sky, and its body solidified before her eyes, distinct features forming from what had a moment before been impossible darkness.

The tall figure before her had a lean, muscled frame with broad shoulders and a narrow waist, and stood completely naked. Those shadowy wings spread wider, and she stared at them in awe—they were like tears in reality, magical windows revealing bright stars and nebulas against a dark purple sky.

His skin was also reminiscent of the night sky, blue-black with thousands of twinkling stars, even upon the gray colored portions making up his chest and face.

And oh God, that face...

It was the face of an angel, or perhaps more accurately, a seductive demon. His features were refined and sharp, with sculpted lips, a straight nose, and defined cheekbones. Thick, arched black brows rested over eyes that now shone brilliant blue and violet against black sclerae and were framed with long, dark lashes.

Short, tousled black locks framed that demonically attractive face, their ends curling roguishly against his forehead, cheeks, and neck. His ears were long and pointed, with silver hoop piercings on their lobes and helixes, each pair of earrings connected by two chains and adorned with a dangling spike. Two black, segmented horns sprouted from his temples, curling backward and up into lethal points.

Holy shit, he was...

"Gorgeous," Ember whispered, unable to take her eyes off the creature.

Those unearthly eyes locked with hers and narrowed. "What did you say?"

Easing forward, she placed her hands on the bed and crawled toward him. She felt an inexplicable pull, a compulsion to be closer to him, to touch him. And she didn't fight it.

He was a monster lover's wet dream come to life. "Are you my wish?"

Frowning, he folded his arms across his chest. A long tail swished through the air behind him. "Your wish, mortal? I am your nightmare."

Ember snorted with a roll of her eyes. "Hardly." She slipped her legs over the edge of the bed and stood.

"Hardly?" Those wings stretched fully, and the room dimmed again, making the light of his eyes stand out even more starkly as he spread his arms in the most *behold me* stance Ember had ever witnessed in person. "I am the void, the vast, lightless emptiness between the stars, the cold embrace of a cosmos your mortal mind cannot fathom."

She smiled as she approached him. "But you're covered in pretty little sparklies."

"Pretty little...?" His eyebrows slanted down sharply, creating a crease between them as he drew in his wings and stepped back from her advance. The moonlight made the silver spike piercings in his nipples glint. He bared his teeth at her, revealing a set of sharp fangs. "What are you doing?"

Ember continued closing the distance between them, the short skirt of her nightgown brushing her bare thighs. "Getting a closer look."

"Stop, mortal. Immediately."

Her smile widened into a grin. "Are you frightened of me?"

"I do not feel fear, I *am* fear. I instill it in creatures like you. You should be cowering in terror, human."

"My name is Ember."

His retreat halted when he bumped into the wall. Scowling, he flattened himself against it as she neared. "I've no need for your name. Let us conclude our business that I may depart this accursed realm."

Ember stopped in front of him, leaving a scant few inches

between them. She was on the taller side at five foot eight, but this creature towered over her. Keeping her eyes on his, she tipped her head back, breathing him in. His scent of spice-infused incense and crisp night sky wrapped around her, suffused her, and teased her senses, causing heat to pool in her now aching core.

This had to be a dream, because there was no way this could be real. No way *he* could be real.

She raised her hands and settled them upon his chest. His nostrils flared with a sharp inhalation. She'd expected him to be insubstantial and cold, but he wasn't. His flesh was solid and warm. She trailed her palms down slowly, over his hard nipples and piercings. "Are you real?"

A shudder coursed through him, and some of the stars on his skin flickered, flaring brighter.

"Of course I'm real." As though reluctant to touch her, he took her wrists between his forefingers and thumbs. His dark claws grazed her skin as he guided her hands away from his chest. "Are you not the one who summoned me, witch?"

Tilting her head, she arched a brow. "Summoned you? Do you mean dreamt you?" She grinned and eased closer to him until her breasts brushed his chest. "Because if this is a dream, I definitely don't want to wake up."

As his gaze dipped to her cleavage, his hold on her wrists tightened, pressing those claws into her skin a little more firmly, and the light in his eyes intensified. "Those are quite...ample..."

He shook himself, lips peeling back to bare those devilish fangs, and narrowed his eyes. "No. I will not fall victim to such wiles again." Tossing her hands aside, he slid along the wall to escape her before stepping forward. "Your charms have no effect on me, witch. Either state your business with me or release me from this summoning."

Ember tried to ignore the sting of rejection as she turned to watch him. She touched her fingers to her chest. If this was a dream, why did that hurt so much? "What are you talking about? And why do you keep calling me a witch?"

His head snapped toward her. "Am I meant to believe this feigned ignorance? That you truly have no notion of what you've done?"

"I was sleeping." Her brow furrowed. "Am sleeping?"

Shaking her head, Ember flicked her wrist, casting her confusion aside. "Anyway, my bed was shaking like there was an earthquake, and there was this bright light coming out from beneath it, then shadows filled the room, and you appeared. Now here we are."

The demon scowled—and damn if that expression didn't look hot as hell on him—before stalking toward her bed. With one hand and seemingly no effort, he dragged her bed away from the wall. A deep, guttural growl rumbled from him as he stared at the floor. "That meddling sprite..."

Ember stepped closer and looked down at what he'd revealed. A circular symbol made of glittering blue-white dust glowed faintly upon the dark wood floorboards, with a pentagram at its center and crescent moons at each of the star's points.

The creature snarled and spun around. "Starling! I know you're lurking nearby. Reveal yourself, now."

A light giggle sounded from thin air. "I have not seen you this lively in so, so long."

Ember's eyes widened as light flashed behind the demon's head, and a glowing orb the same color as the circle floated into view beside him.

But it wasn't an orb at all. It was a lithe, radiant figure, a tiny humanoid with four arms and many-pointed wings formed of sparkling starlight. She had long white hair that glittered as it moved. The sprite bent to whisper loudly in the demon's ear. "I believe the words you are looking for are *thank you, Starling* for finally getting you out of that place, yes?"

The demon closed his eyes, massaged his temples, and exhaled heavily. "What have you done?"

Starling chuckled and turned her head toward Ember. "Oh, I simply taught this lovely witch a little spell while she was sleeping so peacefully. A lunar summoning."

Ember shifted on her feet and crossed her arms over her breasts. "I'm not a witch."

"Oh, but you are!" The sprite darted around Ember before twirling in front of her, flying close enough for Ember to see her face clearly. Starling had delicate elfin features with a sprinkling of alienness. A narrow chin, a tiny nose, and large, glimmering blue eyes with no distinction between sclera and iris. Three of them to be exact, with the third turned vertically at the center of her forehead. Her wide smile revealed razor-sharp, pointed teeth that were fairly unnerving. "A lovely witch who will put an end to his suffering, and thereby mine."

"You taught her to summon me with a *lunar* spell?" the demon demanded, the air around him darkening. "Any other method would've been bad enough, but a lunar summoning? Did you think I would be amused by this? That I would think it a quaint diversion?"

The sprite giggled again. "I am not concerned with what you think about it, only what you do. Because you needed to do something after four hundred years, and it was clear you would not do so on your own."

"It is not your place to decide that."

"Perhaps not," Starling said, shrugging both sets of shoulders. "But it is done, so...enjoy!"

She disappeared. Simply blinked out of existence as though she was never there.

With a growl, the demon's form darkened, and he dissipated into a cloud of shadow. Ember stepped back as the shadows faded like an afterimage from her view. This was it—the dream was over, it was ending in disappointment, and she would wake up feeling worse than she had before going to bed.

Can't even get a man in my dreams.

And then those shadows reappeared, thickening and solidifying to form the demon's body.

He snarled a curse and stormed to the window, which he thrust open fully. Before Ember realized what he meant to do, he leapt out into the night. She heard his huge wings beating the air as she rushed forward.

Bracing her hands on the window frame, she leaned forward and scanned the sky for sign of him. But the demon was either gone or blended in so well that he was effectively invisible.

"That conniving, meddlesome little shit!" the demon growled from behind Ember.

She spun around. Hadn't he just flown out the window? Yet there he was, standing in the center of her bedroom.

His fists were clenched at his sides, his tail swung furiously, and his eyes glowed as bright as stars. Tendrils of shadows lashed the air around him.

"Um... What is going on?" Ember asked.

"My dear friend manipulated you into binding me with a lunar summoning spell," he said tightly. "From this full moon to the next, I am bound to you."

This had to be a dream. There was no way that what she'd seen tonight was real. No way that there was an actual demon in her room, saying he was bound to her. She'd lived in Salem for years, had met all kinds of people, some of whom claimed they were witches or vampires or a host of supernatural creatures, and she'd regularly visited local stores selling items meant for casting spells, charms, and hexes. She loved all of it—all the strangeness, all the imagination and passion, all the occult vibes.

But Ember didn't actually believe in magic.

Wishing upon a star had been a childish gesture. She'd never thought anything would come of it. Only hard work made wishes come true.

So if this was a dream...why not enjoy it before returning to her lonely reality? Especially when this demon was everything she could have ever wanted.

Smiling, Ember walked toward him. "Since we're bound to each other, we could take this time to get to know one another."

"I am a being beyond the limits of human comprehension. And besides"—he raised a finger, pointing at her face—"this is your fault, witch."

Unafraid, she curled her fingers around his and drew it down, not releasing it. "And what do I call you, oh terrifying one?"

His inhuman eyes held hers, searching, those shapely eyebrows still angled down. But he didn't pull away. "You may call me Nyte."

Ember blinked at him. "Nyte. As in...the night sky?"

"Nyte as in Nyte," he replied flatly.

She chuckled and stroked his claw with her thumb. "It's fitting."

Her gaze dropped to his sinful mouth. Stepping closer, she rose on her toes and leaned into him. He tensed and drew back slightly but didn't step away. Instead of kissing him, she moved her mouth to his ear. "There are ways we can get to know each other that my human mind will comprehend very, very well."

Nyte whipped his face toward her, putting his mouth but a whisper away from hers. His gaze dipped to her lips as though he was considering kissing her.

Shutting her eyes, Ember tipped her chin up to press her lips to his.

Before their mouths could make contact, he snarled and ripped away from her. "No. I've had more than my fill of lust, witch, and I will not succumb to yours."

Blinking her eyes open, she watched him stalk to a dark corner. The shadows writhing around him dimmed the stars on his skin, making him appear more ethereal, as he folded his arms across his chest and leaned against the wall. Those blazing eyes very pointedly did not look at her.

Rejected twice. What the hell kind of dream was this? Her ideal fantasy man was right there— *right there*—in front of her, and he didn't even want her. Not only was her dating life a complete failure, but apparently it was the same while she slept. Even her subconscious refused to give her a break!

Maybe this was a nightmare, like he'd said.

She looked at her bed. With a sigh, she placed her hands on it and shoved it back toward the wall beneath the window. The metal frame scraped loudly over the wood floor. When her foot bumped into something, she looked down to find the fallen book. Ember picked it up and set it on the nightstand.

Climbing into bed, she closed the window and lay back, drawing the covers over her legs and up her body. She curled up on her side, and her gaze drifted back toward Nyte, who was still looking away from her.

After she awoke in the morning, this dream would fade, and he'd be gone.

There was a tight knot in her chest at that knowledge as her lashes fluttered shut and she drifted to sleep.

Chapter Four

"By all the hells, it is too fucking bright in here!"

That deep voice and the lurching of her mattress as someone climbed onto it wrenched Ember from sleep and forced a gasp from her throat. The bed frame squeaked and rocked.

She quickly sat up, nearly getting hit in the face by a swinging tail, and scooted back to stare in shock at the demon standing on her bed, who spread his arms to grasp the curtains.

In the sunlight, he appeared a touch wispy and insubstantial, his stars dimmed to teeny specks. But from this angle, she had an incredible view of his ass. His rounded, toned ass.

Ember bit the inside of her lip as her gaze traced over his backside and up to the tail at the base of his spine. How could a tail make an ass infinitely sexier?

Nyte yanked the curtains closed. The stars upon his flesh immediately brightened in the ensuing gloom, and his form again seemed solid but for those shadowy wings.

Am I...still dreaming?

To be sure, she pinched her arm. Pain shot through her. Ember's eyes widened.

Nope, not a dream. That meant...last night had been real. That Nyte was real.

Holy shit, she had a demon in her bedroom. In her bed.

"You're...not able to go out in the day?" she asked as he stepped down from her bed, landing as lightly and silently as a cat despite his size.

Nyte turned to face her with a scowl. "Of course I can go out in the daylight. I'm a nocturnus, not a vampire."

God, he was as wickedly beautiful now as he had been last night. Her gaze trekked over his naked body, over every contour of muscle, down to the defined V on his pelvis, which guided her eyes lower still... Except there was nothing else there. No cock, no shadowy tentacle. Nothing but a smooth mound.

Then his words registered, and Ember gaped at him. "Vampires exist too?"

With a dramatically exasperated sigh, he brought a hand to his forehead. "You are severely uneducated for a witch."

She narrowed her eyes. "For one, I didn't even know I was a witch. And two"—she grabbed one of her pillows and chucked it at him—"just because I didn't know something exists doesn't make me uneducated."

Nyte's hand shot up, catching the pillow with a dull *thump* before it could hit him in the face, and he tossed it back onto the bed with a nonchalant flick of his wrist. He studied her, jaw muscles ticking. "You have been bold in your dealings with me, mortal. Unafraid. Has the human world grown so ignorant in my absence that your kind no longer fears the things that should make your souls icy with terror?"

"Well, I'm not really the religious sort, sooo... I don't really believe in the whole concept of heaven and hell. That also doesn't make me ignorant. Demons, vampires, faeries, monsters under the bed, and all the things that go bump in the night only exist in stories. Or at least they're supposed to. Because obviously you're standing here, very, very real."

Mimicking his pose from the night before, he spread his wings and arms to the sides, and his features darkened, making his violet-blue eyes seem brighter in contrast. "And shouldn't your beliefs be shaken to their core now? Shouldn't my presence, my existence, strike fear into you? Seeing what you thought unreal and impossible, basking in my presence?"

Her lips stretched into a slow smile. He was quite adorable when he acted all grand and powerful. She leaned forward, propped her elbows on her knees, and rested her chin atop her palms. "Actually, I just want to lick you all over."

His arms and wings dropped, and he shook his head, a crease forming between his brows. "What is wrong with you?"

Ember pointed a finger at him. "Hey! There is nothing wrong with me finding a demon, especially one with sparklies all over his skin, sexy."

Nyte stepped toward her, raising his hands with fingers curled to display the black claws at their tips. "I could rend the flesh from your bones and make you feel every agonizing instant of it, little witch. I could overwhelm you with such pain that you would forget who you were and offer to pay any price, even your soul itself, just to make it stop. I could feast upon your entrails as you watched."

Ember arched a brow. "Will you?"

Those sinful lips pressed together, and her heart pounded as he stared at her, his gaze intense, smoldering, otherworldly. Straightening, he folded his arms across his chest and turned his face away, chin lifted haughtily. He hesitated before murmuring, "No."

She chuckled as she flipped the covers aside and slid off the bed to stand. "Then I have nothing to fear from my pretty sparkly demon."

He raked his hands down his face with a grumble. "I am neither pretty nor sparkly, damn it."

"Ah, so you are mine then?"

Nyte glared at her. "I belong to no one."

Ember closed the distance between them and reached up, lightly running the tip of her finger along his jaw. Something changed in his eyes, their light becoming more of a gleam than a shine, and his nostrils flared with a deep inhalation. But he didn't retreat or bat her hand away.

"No, you don't. But you *are* sparkly and pretty." After stroking his chin with her thumb, she dropped her hand and made her way toward the bathroom.

"Where are you going?" he demanded.

"To shower." She paused in the doorway and looked back at him with a coy smile. "You could join me if you'd like, Nyte."

His lips peeled back to bare his fangs. "No."

"I thought you'd say that." She closed the door behind her.

under the bed, and all the things that go bump in the night only exist in stories. Or at least they're supposed to. Because obviously you're standing here, very, very real."

Mimicking his pose from the night before, he spread his wings and arms to the sides, and his features darkened, making his violet-blue eyes seem brighter in contrast. "And shouldn't your beliefs be shaken to their core now? Shouldn't my presence, my existence, strike fear into you? Seeing what you thought unreal and impossible, basking in my presence?"

Her lips stretched into a slow smile. He was quite adorable when he acted all grand and powerful. She leaned forward, propped her elbows on her knees, and rested her chin atop her palms. "Actually, I just want to lick you all over."

His arms and wings dropped, and he shook his head, a crease forming between his brows. "What is wrong with you?"

Ember pointed a finger at him. "Hey! There is nothing wrong with me finding a demon, especially one with sparklies all over his skin, sexy."

Nyte stepped toward her, raising his hands with fingers curled to display the black claws at their tips. "I could rend the flesh from your bones and make you feel every agonizing instant of it, little witch. I could overwhelm you with such pain that you would forget who you were and offer to pay any price, even your soul itself, just to make it stop. I could feast upon your entrails as you watched."

Ember arched a brow. "Will you?"

Those sinful lips pressed together, and her heart pounded as he stared at her, his gaze intense, smoldering, otherworldly. Straightening, he folded his arms across his chest and turned his face away, chin lifted haughtily. He hesitated before murmuring, "No."

She chuckled as she flipped the covers aside and slid off the bed to stand. "Then I have nothing to fear from my pretty sparkly demon."

He raked his hands down his face with a grumble. "I am neither pretty nor sparkly, damn it."

"Ah, so you are mine then?"

Nyte glared at her. "I belong to no one."

Ember closed the distance between them and reached up, lightly running the tip of her finger along his jaw. Something changed in his eyes, their light becoming more of a gleam than a shine, and his nostrils flared with a deep inhalation. But he didn't retreat or bat her hand away.

"No, you don't. But you *are* sparkly and pretty." After stroking his chin with her thumb, she dropped her hand and made her way toward the bathroom.

"Where are you going?" he demanded.

"To shower." She paused in the doorway and looked back at him with a coy smile. "You could join me if you'd like, Nyte."

His lips peeled back to bare his fangs. "No."

"I thought you'd say that." She closed the door behind her.

Chapter Five

Nyte clenched his fists, digging his claws into his palms as he stared at the door.

You could join me if you'd like, Nyte.

Ember's complete lack of fear had been jarring enough, but her forwardness was even more so. Though she'd claimed she hadn't known she was a witch, how could he believe her when her charms were as potent as those of a succubus? Why would she be so open in her interest if not for some nefarious purpose? Humans dealt with demons to obtain power—to make deals, to forge pacts, to gain materials and forbidden knowledge so they could work more powerful magic than their mortal vessels could normally wield.

The most ambitious of them sometimes even tried to enslave beings like Nyte. To bind them with spells, to control them and use them as limitless sources of power.

This was different. Ember was different. She'd not yet asserted any such claim on him, and that had left him embarrassingly off balance thus far. He was the immortal being here, he was the one with the magic, the power. She didn't even know the restrictions placed upon him by the summoning spell! And still she was the one in control.

Nyte growled, glaring at the floor under the bed. Though the summoning circle had faded during the night, it was emblazoned in his memory, and he could almost see it there now, taunting him with its light.

Hells, but he had fallen. The way he'd retreated from her... *He*, a timeless demon coalesced from the night itself, had retreated from *her*, a mortal witch who didn't even know what she was!

His tail whipped behind him, its end striking his leg with a painful sting. With a hiss, he forced it to still.

The sound of falling water came from behind the closed door. His attention snapped back toward it.

The shower. After she'd fallen asleep as though a nocturnus weren't lurking in the corner of her bedroom, Nyte had tested the limits of the binding and explored his surroundings, including the privy. Though there were familiar features in her home, they were greatly outweighed by the strange and new. Even the tub and wash basin were different.

Strangest of all was the thin little box she'd kept on the stand beside her bed all night. It had lit up a few times, casting its glow on the ceiling, and when Nyte had investigated it, there'd been writing on its face. He understood the words, but their meaning eluded him.

Update has been applied successfully. Swipe up to get started.

He'd refused to touch the thing. He was in no mood to inadvertently trigger the scrying mirror—or whatever it was— and make his presence known to some witch on the other side who actually knew what they were doing.

The tone of the shower changed, suggesting that Ember had just stepped beneath the flow.

Did that mean she'd undressed? That she'd slid her nightgown off, revealing more of that smooth skin, more of those enticing curves? Was water now cascading over her full breasts, down her belly, along her long legs?

He'd rejected her invitation, but he was tempted to rematerialize on the other side of that door and enter the tub with her, to behold her body and run his hands over every inch of its softness.

Something stirred low in his belly, something he hadn't felt in centuries. A hot, raw, primal thing beyond his comprehension that had come very close to seizing control whenever she'd touched him.

By the void, the feel of her hands on his skin was unlike anything he'd ever experienced. Even the stroke of her finger along his jaw had left him tingling.

There was no denying it. He wanted the witch.

His tail flicked back and forth eagerly. Growling, he swept a hand backward, catching hold of the rebellious appendage and halting its insufferable motion.

Lust. That was all he was feeling now, and he'd been through it before. Where had it led him? What good had it done? The fleeting moments of pleasure and bliss hadn't been worth the torment he'd endured afterward. He would not allow it to get the better of him again, especially not with a mortal.

And he knew exactly who to blame for all this.

"Starling, show yourself," he snarled, turning away from the privy door.

"Tsk tsk. You are in such a poor temper, Nyte." The sprite's blue-white light appeared beneath the bed, and she flitted up to fly above him tauntingly before landing on his shoulder. Her three eyes met his. "You have a naked woman in there who invited you to join her, and here you are, being snarly."

He scowled at the sprite. "I am not being snarly."

Starling put her four hands on her hips and bared her sharp, pointed teeth. "Starling, show yourself!"

"That is not how I sou—"

She raised her upper hands and clawed at the air. "Grr, grr, hiss, hiss."

Nyte rolled his eyes. "Whenever you're done, you and I need to have a serious conversation."

"Pfft. All you have been is serious for hundreds of years! It is time to move on, Nyte." Starling leapt into the air and hovered before him, waving her arms toward the privy. "She is perfect. I know you can see it as well as I do."

Nyte's tail twitched in his hand, agreeing with the sprite's assessment. He squeezed it. "How do I break the tether?"

"There is no breaking it. You must let it run its course." She tilted her head far, far to the side, practically bending herself in half. "Unless...one of you dies."

"And you know full well that your little binding spell prevents me from doing her harm."

"Of course I know! And I would be very, very cross with you if you were to allow harm to befall our witchling."

"*Our* witchling, is she?"

Starling grinned. "Yes. At least until you make her yours."

"It will not happen. All you've done is condemn me to a month of suffering."

"If you are so averse to getting closer to Ember, you still have two hands. Only you can ease that suffering."

Nyte glared at his companion. "That is not what I meant, and you know it."

Starling clapped her hands with a giggle. "Oh, this will be so entertaining!"

He threw his tail back and leveled a finger at the sprite. "This is cruel. Our friendship has endured for eons, and this is what it's become?"

"It is because I am your friend that I am doing this." She flitted closer, hands on her hips once more, and glared at him. "You have sulked for far too long over someone who did not deserve what you gave her."

"And she certainly didn't deserve what she took, either." Nyte absently rubbed at his chest as the ghost of that old ache stirred within him. "But why, *why*, would you think this mortal is the answer? She didn't even know she's a witch, damn it."

Starling waved a hand. "Her magic is untapped, and that is all the better for you, is it not? If she does not know any spells, she cannot use them against you. As for why her...well, that is for you to discover, Nyte."

"I will not repeat my mistake, Starling. I will not succumb again."

"And I will not allow you to wallow in despair for the rest of your immortal life." She notched her chin up. "Besides, I do not make mistakes. She will not be a mistake."

"Oh, I'm sure I can list at least—"

The shower turned off, and Nyte's attention returned to the closed door. Half-formed images teased at the edges of his mind, imaginings of Ember's naked body, glistening with drops of water as she stepped out of the tub...

He growled through his teeth and swung his gaze back to Starling, only to find empty air where she'd been hovering. "Damn you. You know I've always found that rude."

Faint, tinkling laughter answered him from somewhere unseen.

Nyte balled his fists and drew his wings in tight, tail whipping in agitation. The sprite knew how to break this binding, how to reverse the summoning, she had to know, but she'd never tell him how. She'd never been one to give up once she'd put a plan into motion. Especially if it meant she'd be able to laugh at his expense.

Compose yourself. You cannot allow the mortal to see you in this state.

He'd already been caught off guard by Ember. He could allow himself no further slip-ups, could display no further weakness. She was a human, a witch who knew nothing of magic, and he was the embodiment of the night.

Whatever the terms of this binding, Nyte held the power. The situation was his to control, Starling be damned. He would not allow this mortal witch to—

The privy door opened, and Ember stepped out wearing nothing but the large blue towel wrapped around her lush body.

Fuuuuuuuuck.

Nyte stared at her, unable to look away. Her silver hair was twisted up and clipped high on her head, with damp, loose strands sticking to her neck, and her pale skin was rosy from the heat of the water. All he needed to do was rip that towel away and she'd be bare for his eyes to feast upon.

What color were her nipples? What did her cunt look like? What did it *taste* like?

Heat flared deep inside him and spread through his body, brightening the stars shining through his skin. The magic that fueled him, that formed him, roiled and gathered at his groin, threatening to take shape. Pressure built, thrumming, agonizing pressure, and he knew that if he allowed his cock to form, he'd be lost. He'd take this witch, take everything he wanted from her, and give her everything she wanted in return.

Was he really willing to submit to this lust just for a taste of her?

Ember stopped a couple feet away and smiled as she toyed with the tucked-in corner of the towel, securing the cloth around her. "If you want to see me naked, you only need to say so, Nyte."

Fuck, the way she said his name, caressing it with her soft, sweet voice, would be his undoing.

With a growl, he spun away from her, giving her his back. "Beguiling witch."

His tail swished back and forth behind him. He reached back and caught it, clutching it tight and wishing he could strangle the misbehaving appendage into submission.

Ember chuckled, and he heard her footsteps padding away from him. "I'll take that as a compliment."

Glad for the distance, Nyte drew in a deep breath to calm himself, only to be struck by her fragrance. Enticing gardenia, warm vanilla, and something beneath those notes that was wholly her. He bared his clenched teeth, squeezed his tail, and dug his toe claws into the floorboards as her scent flooded him.

There was a soft *thump* of cloth hitting the floor. The towel.

Ember was unclothed behind him, begging for his hungry gaze, tempting him, torturing him. Beckoning him to turn and behold her. Licks of heat coursed up his spine and through his wings, as though she were a fire giving off the warmth he so desperately needed.

He refused to turn. He would not give in to that urge, would not indulge these base desires.

Movement in front of him drew his eye. Everything in Nyte stilled.

A vanity stood against the wall, and Ember's reflection was in profile in the tall mirror attached to it. If he thought he'd been suffering already, it had been nothing compared to what he felt at seeing her curvy body on display.

As she pulled open the top drawer of her dresser, Nyte's gaze raked over her, from her bare feet with their gray painted toenails, up her legs, and along those delectable thighs to her shapely hips and rounded ass. Nyte gritted his teeth as he fought back the urge to bite it, to mark it. His eyes continued upward, stopping on her large breasts, which were tipped with pink nipples. He craved to draw one into his mouth, wondering what sounds he might wring from her as he teased it with lips, tongue, and fangs.

She turned, and before she bent over to draw on her lacy underwear, he glimpsed the slit of her bare cunt.

His nostrils flared as he tried to maintain control and remain in place. It would be easy to overcome her, to shove her onto her back and spread her thick thighs to see the delicate flesh between them.

The fire within him blazed hotter, and the ache in his groin intensified, railing against his restraint.

When Ember drew on another lacy garment that covered her breasts, he mourned the loss and found himself battling a new impulse to stride over to her and tear that fabric away. Somehow, he kept his feet rooted.

His tail, however, battled fiercely, tugging at the hand still wrapped around it with more force than seemed possible.

Infernal thing.

But the distraction it provided proved just enough for him to finally pry his attention away from the mirror, away from Ember. He swung his gaze toward her bed, staring instead at the window over it. Sunlight bled in around the edges of the curtains. Perhaps if he stared long enough, it would blind him, and he wouldn't have to endure such visual temptation again.

Then there'd only be her bewitching scent, her warm, soothing touch, and the delightful sound of her voice to taunt him.

He heard her open a door, heard cloth rustling and whispering against her skin, and he forced his eyes shut, not that it could block out the visions of her now etched forever into his memory.

"It's safe," Ember said.

Safe? So long as this inferno of lust rages inside me, neither of us is safe.

Seemingly unaware of his turmoil, Ember stepped past him to the vanity. She sat on the stool and flicked a switch. The lights surrounding the mirror flared to life, bright enough that he had to briefly slit his eyes and turn away.

"So light doesn't hurt you, but you're sensitive to it?" she asked.

"I simply need a moment to adjust. A bit of warning would've been appreciated."

"I'll be sure to do that next time." She met his gaze within the mirror before opening one of the drawers and removing a few items, setting them atop the vanity. "How old are you?"

"How old is the night?" Nyte strode to her bed and sat down on its edge, looking her over. She'd put on a black lace dress with a low neckline. The inner skirt was shorter, revealing her legs beneath the long, sheer, lace-embroidered outer layer. Though he'd just seen what lay beneath her clothing, the way the fabric hugged her body, the way it accentuated some of her curves while hiding others, was as tantalizing as her naked form.

No one, especially not a mortal, had any right to be so beautiful.

"So what are you saying? That you're billions of years old?" Ember asked with not a little bit of disbelief.

"I have existed since time immemorial. But awareness came much later, along with this form."

"Wow. You're *old* old."

"By your reckoning, yes. But time flows differently for immortal beings."

"I'm still trying to wrap my mind around this not being a dream." She lifted one of the bottles, opened it, and began applying the skin-colored cream inside to her face with a tiny pink sponge. "What did you mean when you said your awareness and form came later?"

He snatched up a pillow, taking it between both hands. One of her long, silver hairs lay upon it. "It is not something easily explained. I coalesced from the night. I am a manifestation of it. For a long, long while, I was...a force. An entity. Formless power, drifting through the darkness. Feeding on fear. Gradually, that fear shaped me, and as I became aware of myself, so too did this form come into being. A mirror held to humankind's fear of the dark and the unknown."

She met his gaze in the mirror with a grin as she set down the bottle and sponge. "You're not scary looking to me."

"You've made that abundantly clear, witch."

Chuckling, she picked up another item along with a small, soft brush and applied powder to her skin. "I was never scared of the dark. I actually...find comfort in it. I grew up on a farm, and when I was little and couldn't sleep at night, I'd sneak outside and listen to the crickets chirping while I stared up at the stars. It was peaceful."

"There is a certain comfort to be found in the night's music. Those songs the sun will never hear, whispered beneath moon and stars..." Nyte plucked the hair off the pillow, rubbing it between his fingers. He felt a sudden urge to stroke her silken strands, to tuck them behind her ears, to feel their ends tease his skin. Barely holding back a growl, he released the hair, letting it fall away, and returned his gaze to the female who was the focus of these unwelcome desires.

Ember was now coloring her eyelids.

"Why are you painting your face?" he asked.

She paused, drawing the thin brush away to look at it, then at her reflection, before finally turning her face toward him. "My makeup?"

"Yes. Why apply that paint—that makeup—to your face? It's unnecessary."

Her lips curled into a wide smile. "Are you saying I'm pretty, Nyte?"

His eyebrows fell. "You are...not unappealing."

She laughed and shook her head. "I'm assuming you don't freely give out compliments, so I'll take that as one." Ember turned back to the mirror and moved the brush back to her eyelid, adding a touch of purple to the black she'd already applied. "I just like wearing it. It's a way to express myself."

The contrast between the darker colors blended on her eyelids and the light blue of her irises made her eyes ethereal and mesmerizing. To keep from staring into them, from losing himself in them, Nyte dropped his gaze to the pillow. Her fragrance was everywhere in this room, but here on the bed, it was strongest of all.

This was where she slept. Where she was at her most serene, her most vulnerable, where the covers caressed her skin, where she dreamed.

Something sparked within him. Another impulse, this one too quick, too powerful, to deny. Nyte raised the pillow to his face and inhaled deeply. Ember's sweet scent flooded his nose, washing over him to haze his mind.

"Are there others like you?" Ember asked.

Her question pierced that haze; only then did he realize what he'd done, and that his tail was thumping atop the bed.

Biting back a snarl, he tossed the pillow aside and let out a huff as he tucked his tail beneath his thigh. This would be the longest month of his existence if things continued like this.

He shoved himself to his feet and moved away from the bed, away from that concentrated, enthralling scent. "Yes, there are other nocturni."

Ember turned on the stool to look at him. "And since you're not born, I'm assuming you don't reproduce like humans?"

"We do not reproduce at all."

"So does that mean you don't have a..." Her gaze dropped to his groin.

Nyte blinked at her. There was a weight to her words, amplified by her pointed stare. Hers was not an innocent curiosity.

"I am formed of the very essence of the night. Every part of me shaped from it, free to be made or unmade. Physical form is a matter of will for the likes of me, not of being."

Her eyes flared. "You can...summon a dick?"

"Should I so desire, yes."

"Oh my God, really?" She grinned. "Can I see it?"

"I am not a spectacle, witch. I am here neither to entertain you nor to pleasure you."

I'm here because that damnable sprite thinks she knows what is best for me!

Ember stuck her plump bottom lip out in a pout. The expression drove straight into Nyte's core, and it was nearly enough to convince him to acquiesce to her request. Nearly.

He thrust a finger at her with a glare. "I will not be swayed by your charms."

She smirked and turned back to the vanity mirror, picking up a long object and unscrewing it. "I'll have to keep working on them then, since I'm this supposed witch."

Nyte forced himself to spin away from her. By the hells, he was hardly able to resist her already. How was he going to endure until the next full moon?

"What suffering was Starling referring to?" Ember asked.

He gritted his teeth. Starling had spoken far too openly in front of this human, and Nyte had no intention of divulging any details. "That is no concern of yours."

"I'm not trying to pry. I was just curious." There was a pause before she spoke again. "She's your friend?"

"Allegedly."

Ember chuckled. "She seems to want the best for you. How long have you known her?"

"I've known her almost as long as I've been aware. Thousands of years."

"So she's more like a sister?"

A frown tugged down his mouth. His kind were solitary beings, rarely intermingling as they wandered the night. "I cannot say. Such familial relations are not familiar to me."

"Family isn't always blood related. It can be the people you choose. Someone who is close to you, someone who you're comfortable with, who you can share your most treasured secrets and your hurts with. Someone who will always be there for you no matter what happens."

"Does it also involve meddling in my affairs and laughing at my misfortune?"

Ember laughed. "It can. I say this from experience as a middle child with two brothers. They've laughed at my misfortune, and I've meddled with them plenty enough to deserve it. But it all comes from a place of affection."

Her laughter almost coaxed him to look at her again, but he resisted. It was a delightful sound, one that threatened to ease his irritation and make him forget the circumstances currently trapping him.

And it granted him space to ponder her words.

Despite Starling's latest plot, she had always been there for him. Her companionship had been constant, steady, dependable, and supportive. She'd helped him more than he could express and had never given up on him.

Nyte folded his arms across his chest. "Then I suppose my answer is yes. She is like a sister."

"Is she like you? Formed from the night?"

"No. She's fae. A starlight sprite, to be specific. As should be evident, our domains have a bit of overlap."

"How is it that you and all these other supernatural beings exist, really exist, but humans believe you're all just myths?"

He shrugged, waving nonchalantly. "I cannot speak for your kind. Humans knew, long ago, but somehow grew away from that knowledge. My...prolonged absence leaves an unfortunate gap in my knowledge."

"It's still fascinating. Like a whole new world has been opened up to me."

There was a scrape against the floor as she slid her stool back from the vanity and a swish of fabric as she rose.

"All ready!" Ember announced cheerily. "I guess you're coming to work with me today."

Nyte spun on his heel to face her, meaning to refute her assertion and tell her exactly how the day would go, but the words died on his tongue as he beheld her.

Her hair was down, hanging long and loose in waves about her shoulders. Black star earrings with violet centers dangled from her earlobes. And her face...it was beautiful. The makeup didn't mask her features, but accented them. The dark eye paint contrasted both her eyes and her silver hair. But it was the deep, deep shade of violet-red on her lips that drew his attention to her mouth and fixed it there.

He was stricken with the inexplicable need to kiss her. To feel those lips against his, to taste her.

His tail lashed behind him as heat surged through his body.

Fuck. He was worried about making it through the month? How was he going to make it through this *day*?

Chapter Six

With her wide-brimmed black hat perched on her head, Ember slipped her bat winged purse onto her arm, making sure her phone and keys were inside, grabbed her caramel coffee off the kitchen counter, and made her way toward the front door. She opened the door, locked it from the inside, and was about to step over the threshold when she paused, looking over her shoulder at the extremely annoyed demon standing in the dark sitting room beyond the foyer.

Wisps of shadows swirled around him, obscuring his form, but his violet-blue eyes shone brightly within the surrounding darkness.

"Um, will other people see you?" she asked, not in the least bothered by his temper, which had taken a turn after she'd finished getting ready for the day. Something had ruffled him, and he'd clung to his anger since following her downstairs.

"No," he replied through his teeth, "because I am not going out there."

Ember rolled her eyes. "You are, because you're apparently stuck with me, and I have to go to work."

"Your mortal affairs are of no consequence to me. I will *not* traipse about on your errands while the sun is in the sky."

"You said it yourself that you're not a vampire, so you'll be okay dealing with the sun for a little while. And whether you like it or not, you're coming with me, because I have bills to pay. I can't just laze about all month doing nothing like an insufferable, high-and-mighty demon."

"I do not laze about doing nothing," he grumbled.

"From what I heard, you've been moping for the last four hundred years."

With a growl, he drew himself up straighter. His wings spread, his tail struck the floor, and the room darkened around him. "I will tolerate no further argument. You will not exit this dwelling, witch."

Ember arched a brow. "Stop me."

"You wouldn't like that."

She lifted her foot.

Nyte narrowed his eyes. "Don't you dare."

She gave him a saccharine smile. "I dare. Now let's see if you can resist following me."

Ember stepped outside, closing the door behind her. His curses were loud enough to hear clearly through the thick wood. Snickering to herself, she walked along the pathway leading to the sidewalk.

She'd made it to the wrought iron fence that surrounded her yard when Nyte suddenly appeared in front of her, looking angry as fuck.

He's looking quite fuckable, too.

But he also looked...diminished. Just a touch insubstantial, like a shadow struggling to exist amidst too much light. Part of her brain insisted that if she were to reach out, her hand would go right through him.

It wouldn't have been the strangest thing to happen over the last twelve hours.

Ember grinned at him. "I knew you couldn't resist me."

"You are vexatious, witch."

"I guess we're a match made in heaven. Or hell." She stepped closer and reached up to run a finger along his jaw. It didn't pass through him. "You're also quite sexy when you're angry."

Nostrils flaring, he huffed.

Dropping her hand, she moved around him and resumed walking. She didn't miss the odd looks she received from the nearby pedestrians. Based on their expressions and how they were looking at her, Ember could only assume they couldn't see Nyte, and she'd appeared to have been talking to empty air. It didn't bother her. This was Salem, where the strange was embraced.

She took a sip of her coffee.

At the corner of her eye, she saw Nyte walking beside her, matching his stride to hers. The irritation radiating from him was more palpable than the wisps of shadow it produced.

And not a soul so much as glanced in his direction.

"They can't see you," she said.

"I don't find myself in a mood to be seen, currently."

"So they could see you if you wanted them to? It's not just because of our...tether that I can?"

"You can only see me now due to that binding. Otherwise, I can only be seen when I choose to be."

Ember tapped her fingers against her insulated mug and peeked up at Nyte. His brows were angled down sharply, his eyes narrowed and staring straight ahead, and his mouth twisted in a scowl. Guilt seeped into her.

She didn't like the fact that he was bound to her against his will, didn't like that he was forced to suffer her presence. But what else could she do? She couldn't sit at home for an entire month. She'd lose the house she just bought and risk losing her boutique on top of it.

"You're...sure the sun doesn't hurt you?" she asked.

"It is a mild nuisance, nothing more," he replied tightly.

Ember nodded, hesitating before saying. "I'm sorry you're stuck with me. It's not what I would have wanted either. I mean, it's not that I don't like you, I do, I really, really do, it's just, well..."

"Neither of us was given a choice." His voice was gentler than it had been since he'd first appeared in her room last night.

She glanced at him again. His features had also softened.

Maybe he doesn't hate me so much, after all.

When they reached the first intersection, Ember stopped. A car with its windows rolled down drove by, music blaring, the bass thumping so powerfully that she felt it in her chest.

Beside her, Nyte waved a hand before his face as though warding off a foul odor. "So, those hideous things are conveyances. Do they all produce such obnoxious sounds and noxious odors when they move?"

"Some of them. You've never seen a car before?" she asked as they crossed the street, following the crosswalk.

"No. I've been away for a long while, as my dear sprite friend implied."

"Away where?"

Jaw tight, he muttered an answer.

"What was that?"

He let out an exasperated sigh. "The Pit of Despair."

"Oh. Oh, I'm so sorry." She frowned. Starling had said Nyte had been suffering, but Ember hadn't even considered it was because of depression. She hadn't even known demons could get depressed. "Depression is hard to overcome."

"Depression?" He scoffed and shook his head, giving her an

incredulous look. "I wasn't depressed, witch. I was *in* the Pit of Despair."

She gaped at him. "Wait, what? That's an actual place?"

"What did you think it was?"

"A figure of speech."

"Mortals can be so foolish."

"We're not the ones with a place called the Pit of Despair. Is it in hell?"

"One of them. Now, do you have any further questions, or may I return to suffering this torturous daylight in relative silence?"

"Oh no, no, no. You're not getting away with telling me there's an actual Pit of Despair, in *one of the hells*, without telling me more. Why were you there?"

He dragged his tongue across his teeth. "Holiday."

Ember snorted. "So you're trying to tell me you were on vacation in the Pit of Despair? I know I don't really know you, but my instinct is to call BS on that."

One of Nyte's dark brows arched. "BS?"

"Bullshit. I'm calling your bluff."

"My affairs are my own, mortal, and are no concern of yours."

"Okay, fair. How long was this holiday of yours? Curious about what kind of benefits demons get—"

"Four hundred years," he grated through bared fangs.

Ember came to a halt, staring at him in utter shock. She didn't even register the people walking past her.

That's where Nyte had been for four hundred years? And he'd been suffering for all that time. What had been done to him? What had driven him there, and why had he stayed for so long? She highly doubted the Pit of Despair was a resort hotel given its name and location.

But it was clear that he didn't want to talk about it, and she had pressed him enough. She'd have to set her curiosity aside and let him tell her in his own time, if he ever decided to do so.

Nyte slowly canted his head. "You have work to attend, do you not?"

Awareness came back to Ember, and she couldn't be sure how long she'd stood there before she regained her composure. "Um, yeah."

They continued onward for fifteen minutes without speaking as she sipped her coffee and caught glimpses of Nyte observing his surroundings. The crowd had grown, especially in this part of town, where many tourist shops were located. Ember's boutique, Darkly Romantic, was tucked away off one of the main roads overlooking the harbor.

When they reached the door to her store, it was five minutes before ten.

Perfect timing.

She unlocked the door and stepped inside. After turning on the lights, she made her way to the counter, where she set down her coffee and tucked her purse away in a locked drawer at the bottom.

"This is your place of work?" Nyte asked.

Ember glanced up to see him wandering between the display tables and racks of clothing, his eyes roaming over the black and purple patterned walls. She smiled as she looked around her store with pride. Elaborate elaborate candelabra sconces, mirrors, and vines of roses decorated the walls, the shelves were filled with handbags, candles, incense, soaps, jewelry, and makeup, and the headless mannequins scattered throughout were adorned in some of the newly arrived attire. The atmosphere was dark and romantic, living up to its namesake.

This place was everything she'd dreamed of.

"It is," she said. "As a teen, I loved trying out different

styles of clothing, and my favorite was this blend whimsical and dark. Flowing fabrics, long skirts, velvet and lace. But since I lived on a farm in the middle of nowhere, Nebraska, there were no stores like this anywhere. I had to put everything together myself. There was a lot of scraping together money to go thrifting and recycling old hand-me-down clothes. My classmates didn't exactly appreciate my fashion sense."

Nyte swept his eyes over the mannequins and made a hum that sounded a hint more intrigued than dismissive. "What was their fashion sense?"

"For most of them, just practical clothing. Jeans and T-shirts, button downs, tennis shoes or sturdy boots. A lot of kids also lived and worked on family farms. But my style was what people call witchcore these days. Not really a popular trend back in my hometown."

He arched a brow, settling his intense gaze upon her. "*Witch*core."

"I swear I didn't know I was a witch! I still don't believe I am one." She wiggled her fingers at him, envisioning sparks flying from them. "See? Nothing."

By his expression, he was neither impressed nor convinced. "And yet here we both stand."

Ember lowered her hands and shrugged. "Doesn't change the fact I didn't know and didn't summon you on purpose." Looking down, she made sure her point of sale system was up and running before walking to the door and flipping the sign to OPEN.

"I...don't blame you, mortal." There was an odd hesitance in his voice that added sincerity to his words.

When she looked at Nyte, his back was to her as he drifted toward the small section of men's attire. He hadn't been looking at her when he'd said those words, but hearing them relieved a pressure in Ember's chest she hadn't even realized had been there. She felt like a weight had been lifted off her.

Though she'd done her best to remain positive in a situation that was beyond either of their control, she'd feared that he hated her for it...or that her innocent wish had brought about his torment.

"I'm not that bad to be around, am I?" she blurted, her face immediately heating.

His gaze flicked toward her. During his brief silence, that pressure returned to her chest, and the warmth in her cheeks intensified. There were so many scathing things he could've said in response, so many ways he could've cut her down, diminished her, destroyed her.

But when he finally replied, the two most unexpected words came from his mouth. "You're not."

Ember let out a long, slow, relieved breath.

So maybe a month in her presence wouldn't be so bad for him, after all. A girl could hope, right?

He lifted a black poet's shirt from the rack, dangling it from his finger by the hanger. "This looks somewhat closer to the popular fashion from when I last walked amongst your kind."

Ember made her way toward him. She plucked a long, black button-up coat from a rack, took the shirt from him, and slipped the hanger within the coat, pairing the garments before holding them up to Nyte. She smiled. "You would look rather dashing in this."

Nyte looked down at himself and flattened a hand against the clothes, pressing them to his body. The corner of his mouth quirked. "You'd enjoy that, wouldn't you? Seeing me dressed like a human?"

"I just think you'd look handsome in it."

He raised his eyes to meet hers, and his brow furrowed. For the second time today, something softened in his face. She could almost feel it in the way he was looking at her—a hint of curiosity, tempered by lingering wariness.

The front door opened, and new voices accompanied the tinkling bell as customers entered.

Ember yanked the hangers away from Nyte, alarm flaring within her before she recalled that others couldn't see him. He was smirking at her, a playful gleam in his otherworldly eyes.

"Behave," she whispered before turning toward the customers. "Welcome to Darkly Romantic."

Chapter Seven

As the sun sank and evening deepened, Nyte realized that he had never in all his long existence spent a day with anyone. Before seeking isolation in the Pit of Despair, he'd spent plenty of nights with company—often with Starling—but his days had always been times of quiet seclusion, awaiting the next sunset.

Though daytime was not the bane of nocturni, it was a mild hindrance. Everything required a little more effort for him during the day, a little more energy, and given that he had eternity stretching before him, he'd always chosen to spend his days in respite.

He never would've believed that a day, any day, could be enjoyable. Tedious? Absolutely. Taxing? Most definitely. Irritating? Without a doubt.

But the time he'd spent with Ember, the day he'd spent with her...

It...hasn't been unpleasant.

From his place in the corner, leaning against the wall beside shelves that held an excessive number of handbags, he watched Ember chat to a patron who was purchasing garments.

Though the sign on the shop's front door clearly stated it would close at six bells past noon, it was now a quarter past six, and the silver-haired proprietress was as warm and friendly as she'd been upon opening.

Ember adored this shop. Her passion was evident in her every interaction with her customers, and it was no less clear during the lulls, when she would lovingly tidy up the goods on display.

Nyte had found it fascinating. Shockingly so.

Mayhap it was because he'd been away from this world for so long. The mundane had become unfamiliar and wondrous after centuries of confinement, and there had ever been a part of him that sought out others, mortal and immortal alike. A part that had always taken comfort in being near other beings.

He didn't need to interact with them—that was often draining and unnecessary. But he'd always enjoyed observing.

His gaze trailed over Ember, seizing on her smile. The dark lip paint made her straight white teeth all the more brilliant in comparison. Her smile was radiant.

Or mayhap it is all due to this little witch.

It was more than the way she ran her shop. Whenever Nyte and Ember had been alone throughout the day, no matter what else she'd busied herself with, she'd taken the time to speak with him. She'd asked him questions about himself with disarmingly unobtrusive gentleness, and more than once had asked if he needed anything.

She, a mortal who knew nothing of his world, had been considerate enough to ask a demon born of the night if he required anything for his comfort and wellbeing.

The first time, he'd been convinced it was some sort of trick. A means of stealing a bit of his trust, of getting him to lower his guard, to expose a vulnerability. Mortals and immortals were both well versed in such tactics of manipulation.

But he was beginning to understand the truth now, and he found that truth far more unsettling.

She was simply...kind. Genuine. Compassionate.

Those traits were almost as foreign to him as this modern human world.

Sarnessa had never been—

No. I will not allow my thoughts to follow that path.

When the sale was finalized, Ember bid the woman a good night, and the customer exited the store.

Nyte pushed away from the wall, moving toward Ember. She offered him a smile before crouching to retrieve her bag from the bottom drawer.

"So, is this how you spend your days?" he asked.

"Yep. Five days a week." She stood and faced him, slipping the straps of her bag over her arm. "Now we can head home."

Home.

Another mortal concept that meant nothing to him, like family. He didn't have a home. Didn't have a place he truly belonged.

He preceded Ember out of the shop, watching people walk along the street as she locked up behind him. There'd been humans out in the morning, but it was much livelier and more crowded now. There were what appeared to be mated couples of varying ages, some of them holding hands, families with rowdy children, and groups of mortals talking amongst themselves. The smells on the air were stronger and more pungent, likely coming from nearby eateries, mixing with the briny scent of the ocean.

Ember and Nyte took the same route as they had that morning, their pace slower due to the abundant humans and the roads being packed with the conveyances she called cars.

"So what did you do before your time in the Pit of Despair?" she asked. "Did you have some unholy rites to perform, or did you possess people and make them vomit pea soup?"

Nyte jerked his head toward her, steps faltering. "What in the hells are you talking about, witch? What does pea soup have to do with anything?"

"It's from an old movie. Guess you were away for that one." She chuckled. "Sorry. You've been away for *every* movie. I'll have to share some with you."

He still wasn't sure how to take her laughter, her interest, her smiles. Wasn't sure how to take Ember herself. She was so nonchalant and natural around him, so comfortable.

But alarmingly, he found himself liking that laughter and those smiles, liking the way her eyes often sought him out, liking her attention. Liking *her*. It was certainly too early to judge, but she treated him as though he mattered. As though she was interested in Nyte himself rather than what he could do for her or what he could give her.

He should've been raging against this situation, should've been seething at being trapped in the mortal realm, tethered to a witch...

Instead, he craved her. That was an ominous portent for the days to come. He knew better than to let his guard down, and yet he was already falling into these feelings. He was already slipping.

Nyte caught hold of his overexcited tail and clutched it as he walked. "Before, I was largely an observer. A shadow in the night. I sowed fear and feasted upon it when the whim took me, but often I was content to merely watch. To exist as the world changed around me, and the mortals changed along with it."

"Is that how you know so much about people?"

He couldn't hold back a snicker. "I fear my knowledge of your kind might be a touch outdated."

"Sure is," she said with a grin. "So you don't possess people?"

With a scoff, he gestured at himself. "Why would I trade this shape to wear mortal flesh?"

"Point taken."

He didn't miss the way her gaze darkened as it raked along his form.

Nor did he miss the way his body reacted to that heated look.

Nyte wound his tail around his fist to keep it still.

When they reached Ember's home, she opened the door, letting him enter before stepping inside and locking it. After she removed her hat and footwear, she made her way back to the kitchen with Nyte trailing her, where she set her handbag down on the counter and took out that thin black box. She tapped on it, shaking her head with a laugh before tapping it again. It vibrated a moment later.

Tilting his head, Nyte watched her interact with it. He'd seen many of the mortals who'd come to her store today using similar objects. It seemed all humans possessed such items. By what magic did it glow from within? The more he observed of this world, the more questions he had. "What is that thing?"

Ember looked up at him and smiled as she turned the box to show him. The front was no longer black, but white with blocks of color. There was a name at the top—Maggie. "It's a cellphone. It's used...well, for a lot of things, but mostly to communicate with other people. I was just texting my friend Maggie. Texting is when you send written messages back and forth to one another."

"With no need for a courier? How can such sorcery be mundane for you, yet you know nothing of inhuman creatures or your own magic?"

"It's not sorcery. It's technology. It's...electronics and wireless signals and wavelengths in the air. But I guess to most of us, it might as well be magic."

Technology... It seemed that even as humanity had regressed in their knowledge of the arcane, they'd greatly advanced in other ways.

"Hmm." Nyte ran his eyes over the writing on the screen, which was far crisper and more uniform than anything he'd seen produced by humans in the past. "Which are your messages?"

When she indicated the right side, he pointed at a message on the left. "This is Maggie asking you how your date went?"

She nodded and set the phone on the counter. The screen was now black. "It is."

"What does she mean by *date*?"

Ember stepped away from him and moved to a tall cabinet. When she opened the doors, light spilled out, revealing shelves stocked with food and drink inside. "A date is something people go on. Usually a couple looking to get to know each other romantically. Sometimes it can be an outing with a friend."

"And which was yours?" he asked as she removed a package and some vegetables, cradling them in her arm.

She closed the doors and placed the items on the counter. "I went on a date with a guy hoping to make a romantic connection."

Nyte froze. Something shifted in his gut, something thick and heavy and cold. He didn't like her answer. Didn't like it at all. He didn't want to hear about her going on a *date* with another male, didn't want to hear about her romantically connecting with anyone else.

The thought of another male putting his hands on her, kissing her, fucking her, enraged him to an unreasonable degree.

Fuck.

How had he gone from wanting nothing to do with her to feeling this in less than a day?

Nyte didn't want to speak the next words that emerged from his mouth, but he couldn't hold them back. "And did you find that connection?"

She scrunched her face and vigorously shook her head. "Hell no. He was an inconsiderate ass who kept calling me Amber. *Amber.*"

"Should he have called you *mortal* or *witch* instead? You seem to enjoy that."

"You're only doing that because you're frustrated about our situation...and because you're a demon. He saw my name on the dating app and had been texting me for a couple weeks prior to our date, but he still got it wrong when we met. When I corrected him, he basically blew me off and got it wrong *again*. A guy should know a girl's name when they're out on a date."

She frowned as she picked up a wooden board and drew a large knife from the block, placing them in front of her. "I've tried so many times to find a partner, and every try has ended the same. It's a real shitty feeling when someone who says they like you turns out to not be interested in you at all...just in what you can do for them. My name wasn't important enough for him to remember, but he went into that date expecting he was going to be rewarded for his time by getting laid."

Ember's words resonated with Nyte far more deeply than he would've expected. Yes, a man getting her name wrong was insignificant compared to what Nyte had suffered, but the core of it was the same. The hurt, though far smaller, was the same. The disappointment and pain of thinking there had been a more meaningful connection only to find out that it had all been superficial, that there'd been ulterior motives...

"Yes, it is a...shitty feeling." Nyte paused for a moment. "What does it mean to get laid?"

She withdrew a tool from a drawer and began skinning the carrot. "To have sex."

"Ah." Everything always came back to that, didn't it? No matter the people, no matter the realm.

"That date was last night, before I made my wish," Ember said without looking at him. There was a crease between her dark brows, one that spoke of...pain. "I wished for love. The fated kind of love that only exists in stories."

She wrinkled her nose, keeping her gaze focused on her task. "I guess Starling overheard me and, well... That's what got us into this mess. A stupid, hopeful wish on a shooting star."

Nyte frowned as he watched her. He didn't want to feel this mortal's sadness, didn't want to empathize with her pain, but how could he stop himself from doing so?

"It wasn't stupid," he said softly.

Ember paused and looked up at him. There was vulnerability within the blue depths of her eyes as they searched his, a loneliness that echoed in the hollow cavern of Nyte's chest. In that moment, he felt something between them, something solid and powerful, something real. Something beyond the spell tethering them together.

She dropped her gaze, breaking that connection as she resumed peeling the carrot. "Maybe not."

Despite his desire to continue staring into her lovely, entrancing eyes, these feelings were...raw, uncomfortable, and unsettling. His arms itched with the want to wrap around her in a tight embrace, to draw her against his chest and soothe her.

But that physical contact would've been too much. The temptation would've broken him.

He tore his gaze away from her and forced his legs into motion, exiting the kitchen and leaving her to her work. It didn't help that her scent was everywhere, but at least he wasn't looking at her now, and examining her home would prevent him from recalling her naked form as he'd spied it in the mirror this morning...

Nyte clenched his fists against the craving to touch her, to explore her soft, curvy body, to feel it against his own.

His tail flicked excitedly behind him.

Gritting his teeth, he caught the blasted thing, tempted to rip the appendage off. It would be much easier to simply will it out of existence, but that wouldn't have quite the visceral impact he needed to distract himself.

He heard the water come on in the kitchen as he entered the drawing room. Only after having been outside and seen some of the city could he recognize the age on display here. Ember's home didn't seem to fit with the other modernities he'd witnessed today. Where they weren't covered by the large, patterned rug, the floorboards were slightly warped and bore a warm patina, suggesting many generations of humans had walked upon them. The green wallpaper, with its gold leaf patterns, was faded, peeling at the seams in some places and bubbling in others.

As Ember's knife clacked against the board with a steady rhythm, Nyte moved to the green settee positioned near the middle of the room. It was thicker and plusher than those he'd seen before, with far more cushion and no visible wood. He brushed his fingers across the back of it. The fabric was textured but surprisingly soft.

The settee faced a stand upon which stood a wide black object that looked very much like Ember's cellphone when it was dark, only manyfold larger. Another artifact for communication, mayhap?

He moved to the black box and tentatively tapped its glassy surface. The sound it made was very much not like glass—and nothing happened. There was no light, no images, no text. Simply blackness.

Lowering his brows, he tapped it again, a little harder this time. The whole thing wobbled.

Eyes widening, he grasped the edges of its narrow frame with both hands, looking toward the kitchen as he steadied the object.

Something sizzled on the other side of the doorway. Several seconds passed, and Ember didn't appear.

Letting out a breath, Nyte carefully released the large device, backed away from it, and went to the fireplace. At least that was a familiar thing. Its header, trim, and pillars were decorated with flowing, elaborate carvings that looked to have been painted over a few times too many, robbing them of some of the depth they must once have had. The bricks backing the firebox were dark with untold years of soot. Above the mantel stood a large mirror with an intricately carved wood frame.

He studied his reflection against the backdrop of the drawing room. However old this house was, Nyte was far older...and he was a thing that did not belong in this world. He was out of place here.

Wasn't he?

His gaze shifted to the reflected settee. Could he see himself sitting there with Ember, chatting? Could he see them there, wrapped in one another's arms, with a fire crackling in the hearth?

Could he find fulfillment and belonging in the trappings of a mortal life?

The pile of boxes against one of the walls caught his attention, and he strode to them. Most had the words *LIVING ROOM* written on their sides in black ink.

Nyte lifted a flap on the top one and looked inside. It contained framed paintings, though their realism and clarity were far beyond anything he'd seen from any painter, like actual moments of time had been plucked from reality and frozen on canvas. He picked up the top painting.

It depicted two young human boys and a girl posing in front of a large, green metal conveyance that only resembled the cars he'd seen outside because of the wheels attached to it. A golden field of wheat stood behind the children.

He recognized Ember by the bright blue of her eyes, though her hair was fully black rather than silver. This was her as a child, and he could only assume the boys were her brothers based on their resemblance.

The sizzling sounds persisted in the kitchen, and aromas drifted to him. He recognized those of cooking garlic and meat, accompanied by something sweet and fragrant.

He set down the first painting and picked up another. It was one of Ember and another woman. The two were leaning into one another in a partial embrace, their smiles wide and bright. The other woman was shorter than Ember, with long red hair, pale skin, dark brown eyes, and red-painted lips. She wore a black gown with lace sleeves and a black veil in her hair, and she was clutching a bouquet of red roses. But it was Ember who captivated Nyte. Her hair was black, cascading over her shoulders in soft curls. She wore a sleeveless red corset dress that cradled her large breasts and cinched at her waist before flowing over her flaring hips.

Beautiful was not adequate enough a word to describe her.

A soft giggle came from over Nyte's left shoulder. "I think you like her."

His muscles tensed, but he caught himself before squeezing the frame too tightly, returning it to its place with deliberate care. "Relative to how much I like you at the moment, yes, I quite like this witch."

Starling flitted to his front, her lips spread in a sharp-toothed smile. "Ha! I knew it, because I know you adore me."

He dragged his tongue across the front of his teeth. "I'll not allow your intentional misconstruing of my words to get under my skin, sprite."

"Oh, do not be so stubborn, Nyte." She flew closer and tapped the tip of his nose. "If you would let go of your distrust and anguish, you would see that Ember could warm that cold heart of yours."

She waggled her brow. "And your bed."

Growling, Nyte shooed the sprite away with a wave of his hand.

Starling laughed and flew out of his reach. "There is nothing wrong with enjoying the fruits of the flesh."

Sex.

It had once been foreign to him. He'd watched others copulate, had even been intrigued by the act—there was something primal about it, something gritty and passionate, something real in a way little else seemed to be. But he'd never experienced it himself, had never felt the urge to do so, not until...*her*. Until Sarnessa. She'd changed him. She'd awoken something within him, made him crave, made him need.

And then she'd left him cold and hollow.

He had no want to experience that icy emptiness again.

But with Ember, that carnal desire had rekindled. Hells, it had been stoked into a damned inferno. He could only imagine the intensity of the cold snap that would follow.

Nyte glared at Starling. "Have you not meddled enough in my affairs, sprite?"

She leveled a finger at him. "You needed some meddling, or you would have continued to waste away in Despair."

With her fluttering wings shedding flecks of star dust that disappeared before they reached the floor, Starling zipped past Nyte to peer around the corner at Ember. He hurried after her, grabbed her by her tiny foot, and dragged her back.

"Hey!" She tugged her foot away and put her four hands on her hips with a glare.

"Oh no, no, no. You've no right to be cross with me, Starling. *I* am cross with *you*. You've cursed me to a month amongst mortals."

"And how much time have you spent amongst mortals in the past? You sorely need to remove the stick from your posterior and see this as a gift. A disruption of your stagnant routine." She tilted her head. "Was today truly so terrible?"

Nyte pressed his lips together, clenching his jaw, because he knew the honest answer to that question, and it didn't require any thought.

No, the day hadn't been terrible. Quite the opposite in fact.

But he sure as hell wasn't about to admit that out loud, especially not to Starling. He'd never hear the end of it.

Without thinking, he leaned aside, peeking around the corner into the kitchen. Ember stood at the stove with her back toward him, fussing over whatever was on the burners. His eyes raked over her body of their own accord, from that long, silvery hair all the way down to her feet.

Void consume him, but she never failed to be a sight to behold.

His gaze locked on the curve of her ass.

That is most definitely a sight to behold.

"You are staring," Starling whispered in his ear. "And how could you not? I would take a bite of *that* fruit."

A growl rose from Nyte's chest, ripping up his throat and forcing its way through his bared fangs. "*Mine.*"

His eyes widened when he realized what he'd said.

Ember turned to look his way. "Nyte?"

He jerked back, ducking out of her view and flattening himself against the wall. Licks of fire crackled out from his heart, pulsing through his chest and pooling in his stomach like scalding magma.

Starling lazily floated in the air nearby, one hand over her mouth and the rest over her stomach, her shoulders shaking as she silently laughed at him.

"Is everything okay?" Ember called.

He mouthed curses at the still laughing sprite before calling, "Yes, witch. No need to concern yourself."

"Okay..."

When he heard the sound of utensils against the metal pan, relief flooded him, nearly making him sag against the wall.

"Well, well, well," Starling said with a self-satisfied grin. "You *do* want our witchling."

Glaring at her, he stalked away from the doorway, ensuring he would be out of Ember's earshot, before turning to face the sprite. "Who or what I desire is of no consequence, you interloping miscreant."

The sprite's grin widened. "That was not a denial..."

He could only sharpen his glare.

Starling's smile fell, and the glee faded from her eyes. Solemnity had ever been rare for her, and it was always jarring when she fell into it, even briefly. "She wished for you, Nyte. You did not hear the longing in her voice, the loneliness."

"She didn't wish for me, Starling. She wished for love."

Starling shook her head. "Not just love." She held out her upper right hand, and a glittering, starlike orb formed above it.

A voice echoed softly from the orb. Ember's voice. "*Starlight, starbright, first star I see tonight. I... I wish for love. A deep, abiding love. A love that's unwavering, unconditional, that's never judgmental. A love that feels...fated. Please, send me someone who I can forever trust with my heart.*"

The orb disappeared, and Starling lowered her hand. "She wished for everything you have longed for. Everything that should have been yours, but was cruelly ripped away from you by that treacherous succubitch."

Emotions roiled in Nyte's chest, old, prickly emotions that had never fully gone to rest. Part of him feared they never would. He shook his head. "The only thing she ripped away was the pretense that any of it was real. That anything I felt was real."

Though Starling was so small, the frown that tugged down her lips was huge. However frustrated he was with her, seeing that expression on her face clawed at Nyte's heart.

She drew her upper hands in, placing them over her chest. "What you felt, what you feel, is real, Nyte. It ever has been."

Oh, he knew some of it was genuine. The pain. The bitterness, the anger. Those emotions lived inside him, alive and well even after so long. But for the first time in centuries, they were overshadowed by something else, by something new. By his feelings for Ember.

The only question was *what* those feelings were.

He released a slow, unsteady breath. These mood swings were like a pendulum, barreling back and forth without regard for anything else, ceaseless and exhausting.

Starling flitted closer and reached out, touching his cheeks. "You are my oldest and dearest friend, Nyte, and I want only what is best for you. I cannot bear to see you suffer in that pit any longer."

"My pain need not be yours, Starling."

"No, but it is all the same. Afford me this favor... Think upon what I have said. Think upon Ember's wish. One cycle of the moon is so small a time for you to give when you have eternity."

The corners of his lips curled up. "I will consider thinking upon your words."

"Good." She pinched his cheeks. "You are so adorable

when you smile. Let her see it, and she will certainly fall in love!"

"Have I ever confessed that I sometimes loathe your company?"

She smirked, eyes sparkling. "Many times. But I know they were lies."

He shook his head and waved her away. "Off with you, then. I've mortal matters to attend."

Starling giggled and disappeared.

Despite what she'd done and the mess she'd left him trapped in, he adored the sprite.

She really is like a sister to me. Just as the witch said.

"Nyte?" Ember called.

He shook his wings, but the gesture could not shed the turmoil within him.

Composed. Confident. In control. I am a nocturnus of old, a being possessing power beyond her fathoming.

Standing straight with his shoulders squared, he walked back to the kitchen entrance. Ember wasn't in sight. He continued through the kitchen, following the direction her voice had come from to find her in a connected dining room. She stood beside a round table upon which two plates of food had been set, each paired with a glass of water.

"What is this?" he asked as he approached her.

She gestured to one of the plates. "I made spaghetti Bolognese."

"Are those words intended to mean anything to me?"

"It's food. You eat it."

Nyte stopped behind the chair near the plate she'd indicated, staring down at the food. Long noodles covered in red sauce with meat and vegetables mixed in. "I don't eat human slop."

"Wow. Okay. That's not a very nice thing to say."

His brow furrowed, and he looked at Ember. She was glaring at him with a gleam of hurt in her eyes.

"I've told you, witch, that I feed on fear."

"Yeah, well, I didn't know that was all you ate." She picked up the plate and turned toward the kitchen. "That's fine. If you don't want this *slop*, you don't have to eat it."

This brief stay in the world of mortals had introduced him to many things he did not understand, but this exchange was perhaps the most perplexing—and by far the most distressing. Seeing her upset did something to Nyte. It felt like a taloned hand had reached into his chest, grasped everything within it, and twisted it all into knots.

She cooked this food. She put time, effort, and thought into it, and she wanted to share it with me.

And he'd insulted it. Had insulted her.

Nyte darted in front of Ember before she could reach the kitchen. Eyes flaring, she halted with a gasp.

He took the plate from her. "No. You made this for me, so it is mine."

Mine.

There was that word again. It echoed through him as their eyes met, thrumming into every part of his being.

He grasped her wrist with his free hand and led her back to the table, struggling to keep from focusing on the warmth and softness of her skin. Returning his plate to its place, he dragged out the chair from her spot and pointed to it. "Sit."

She blinked at him with wide eyes and sat.

"Good witch," Nyte said huskily, and his chest heated when her cheeks pinkened and her lips parted with a sharp inhalation.

Something about her reaction, her obedience, was...thrilling to him. But he could not explore that feeling, could not allow himself to fall into it.

He took his seat next to her and stared down at the food piled upon his plate. His tail twitched behind him through the opening of the chair. A fork lay beside the plate, set atop a paper napkin. He'd seen humans eat countless times, had seen them use their hands and all manner of utensils, but that didn't diminish the strangeness of sitting at a table himself with steaming food in front of him.

Food that had been prepared for him.

Taking the fork in his fist, he poked the tines into the mound of noodles and scooped a wad of them up. They dangled from the utensil, dripping sauce onto the plate. He lifted it higher, frowning at the wiggly food.

So undignified.

Nyte bent his head down and brought the spaghetti Bolognese to his mouth. Noodles brushed his lips, painting them with sauce, so he opened them wider and extended his tongue, seeking to hook the noodles and draw them into his mouth. More sauce splattered his chin before he closed his mouth around the bite.

A soft laugh escaped from Ember.

Sliding the fork free, he shot her a glare.

She picked up a napkin, and with gentle strokes, wiped the sauce from his face. "I guess you've never eaten human food before, have you?"

He shook his head distractedly as he regarded her. He should've felt patronized by what she'd just done, should've been insulted by the implication that he could not clean himself, but he felt only...cared for.

Yet another disarming feeling in this mortal's presence.

But he was afforded no time to dwell upon that, because the flavor struck him all at once. It was intense and complex, comprised of so many little parts, and yet each piece complemented the others to create a harmonious whole.

Tentatively, he chewed. The feel of the food in his mouth, being crushed by his teeth, was undeniably odd. But the experience wasn't unpleasant. In fact, the texture of the food somehow enhanced the taste. An appreciative hum rumbled from him.

Ember grinned. "You like it?"

With a nod, he swallowed the mouthful, jabbed his fork into the pile, and shoveled more into his mouth. He barely noticed the sauce splattering his skin this time. It didn't matter.

Like Starling had said, he had eternity. Cleanup could come later.

Ember chuckled and picked up her fork. "Here. Like this."

She stuck the fork into the pile of pasta and twirled it, wrapping the noodles around the tines. When she lifted it, most of the spaghetti was wound in a bundle, with only a couple short ends dangling. Far neater than his attempts.

Ember brought the fork to her mouth, and Nyte watched her lips as they parted, as she slipped the food past them, as they closed around the utensil before she pulled it free.

That heat inside him intensified, burning like the sun at the center of his chest. Those lips looked so soft, so pliable, so tender. He had to fight to keep from envisioning them wrapping around something else. Had to fight to keep from wondering what they would feel like against his skin.

Her pink tongue slipped out to lick a spot of sauce away from the corner of her mouth.

He forced his eyes away and focused on his food, mimicking her technique to scoop up another forkful of pasta. It was the only way to keep his thoughts from straying down another path.

But he could not hide from the understanding that such flimsy distractions would not long hold his growing desires at bay.

Chapter Eight

When Ember emerged from the privy, her face was free of makeup, and she was wearing a short, black satin and lace nightdress that left very little to the imagination. Nyte's legs tensed as though they'd decided on their own to carry him toward her, but he willed his feet to remain in place, keeping his back against the wall and his arms across his chest.

There was so much of that lovely skin exposed.

He gritted his teeth and curled his claws into his arms. His tail, that wretched thing, happily wagged behind him. He pressed himself more firmly to the wall, pinning the appendage in place.

Ember raised her arms over her head and gathered her hair. The action lifted the hem of the nightdress higher on her thighs and made the fabric mold to her breasts.

Nyte's gaze roamed up those long legs and fixed upon her chest, where he could see the outlines of her nipples.

Fuck.

Overwhelming sensations buzzed low in his belly and down into his pelvis. At this rate, his cock was going to form whether he wanted it to or not. Hells, he could almost feel it even now, could almost feel it twitching with pressure and anticipation.

"You can sleep beside me in bed," she said as she walked past him, securing her hair atop her head in a messy bun.

Nyte's eyes fixated on her ass, tracing its luscious curve.

And then her words registered. Lie beside her through the night?

Yes.

"No," he said curtly.

She looked back at him with a cheeky smile. "Why not? Scared I might bite?"

To his frustration, part of him longed to learn the feel of her teeth marking him. "I don't sleep, witch."

"Oh. Don't you ever get bored?"

"How could I get bored when there are infinite universal mysteries to contemplate?"

She smirked. "Soooo...that's a yes?"

He let out a huff through his nostrils. "Occasionally."

"Hmm... Ah-ha!" She moved to her nightstand and picked up a thin, rectangular object.

Nyte had to restrain his excitement as she approached him, especially as her sweet gardenia and vanilla scent flooded his senses. He could not allow her nearness to affect him. Would not.

But as she stood next to him and opened the object, he could feel the heat radiating from her, beckoning him closer, intensifying the ache in his groin.

Ember tapped a button, and the screen on the upper half lit up. It was reminiscent of her cellphone and the display on the counter in her store, but larger. The lower portion of the object had many buttons with glowing numbers and letters upon them.

"This is a laptop. A portable computer." She used the small, flat pad to move a tiny arrow around the screen. "If you double click this icon, you can watch movies." She moved the arrow to another tiny image. "If you open this one, you can browse the internet, allowing you to search anything and everything you can think of."

Ember looked up at him. "Might help you catch up on things in the modern world since you're four hundred years behind."

Nyte's gaze flicked from Ember to the screen. "Show me."

She clicked on the icon she called the internet and a new screen appeared. Then she pressed down on the lettered buttons like they were the keys of a harpsichord. One letter at a time, the word *demon* came onto the screen, and then she tapped a button that read ENTER. The screen immediately changed to another that described what a demon was, with religious and mythological stories tied to them and images of varying horned creatures.

"I've never seen a means of scrying that could produce information like this," Nyte said as he looked over the text. "Though I cannot say if it is much use. Most of this is wildly incorrect."

"Then I shouldn't have to press it upon you to not believe everything you read on the internet." Ember smiled and passed him the laptop. "You can look up current events to learn about how the world has changed from what you knew, or just...put on some movies and be entertained."

She stepped away from him, and Nyte watched her go, resisting the urge to grab her and draw her back to his side.

Peeling back the covers, she climbed onto the bed and slipped beneath them before she reached over to turn off the lamp on the nightstand, plunging the room into darkness. The only remaining light came from the laptop's screen and the faint glow of the streetlamps outside, which crept in around the edges of the curtains.

But Nyte saw perfectly in the darkness. He watched his witch as she lay down on her side and drew the blanket over her.

"Goodnight, Nyte," she said softly, closing her eyes.

"Goodnight, witch," he replied just as gently.

Some part of him would've been content to keep his gaze upon her, but he forced his attention to the laptop. It didn't matter that the empty space in her bed was a void his body could perfectly have filled, didn't matter how tempting the thought of lying beside her, wrapping her in his arms, and tucking her body against his was.

He dissipated his wings and sank down to sit on the floor, leaning back against the wall and holding the laptop on his lap. Based on its name, he assumed that was the intended method of use.

Nyte hesitated with his fingers hovering over the lettered keys. She'd said he could search anything and everything he could think of. How was one to narrow infinite options into a single choice? If he could look up information on anything, anything in all creation, what should he begin with?

His eyeballs itched to shift back toward the bed, but he kept them focused downward as his fingers set into slow, deliberate motion, pressing the keys.

E-M-B-E-R

He tapped *ENTER* like she'd demonstrated. The screen changed, but to his disappointment, there was nothing about Ember. Only the definition of the word, a list of locations that bore it in their names, and a few images of red and orange glowing coals.

Where was his witch? How could he find out more about her?

With painstaking concentration, he tried to move the little arrow to the box he'd written inside. After several tries, he finally determined the angle at which he had to hold his finger so his claw wouldn't interfere with the strange pad.

He added another word to his search.

EMBER WITCH

This time, different images appeared—women in pointed hats wielding fire. None of them even remotely resembled his Ember.

Frowning, he let his eyes roam over the laptop. It was a strange thing, undoubtedly, but it possessed a wondrousness that could not be denied. Her granting him its use had been an opportunity, and he was determined to make the most of it.

If he could not learn about the woman who'd summoned him, he would learn about her world instead. He knew his time here would be far more bearable if he was more familiar with his surroundings.

He began with a simple but important question, though the question mark took no small amount of fiddling to produce, as the key it was printed on seemed predisposed to creating a slash symbol on the screen.

WHERE AM I?

His education on the modern world began with reading about the town of Salem, Massachusetts and its four hundred years of history. It seemed somehow fitting that the place Ember called home had existed for nearly the same length of time Nyte had been gone.

He read about the infamous witch trials, in which nineteen people had been hanged, one man had been pressed to death under stones, and five others had perished due to poor conditions in the jails holding them. Death was part of the mortal world. Nyte had never given it much thought; countless humans had died during his existence, more than he could ever count, and some of those lives had been claimed by his own hands. But these deaths stood out to him, as none of the accused seemed to have been actual witches—nor had they been guilty of the alleged crimes.

Was the abundance of witch-related shops and décor in the town now a reaction to that injustice?

The information on Salem shifted to its role as an important port city in the centuries following that dark chapter, having dealt in significant international trade. But as shipping interests had shifted to larger cities, the town had changed its focus to manufacturing.

It seemed this place was a prime example of the way human technology and interests had been in flux for all the years Nyte had been gone, how their civilization changed as swiftly and frequently as the wind.

Nyte expanded his searches from there, sometimes following trails of information as they veered into different subjects, sometimes exploring things he'd seen or heard during the day with Ember. He devoured the information with surprising ravenousness. He'd spent so long observing the human world, and he must've forgotten just how fascinating he'd always found it during his self-imposed exile.

Only when a soft moan broke the silence in the room did he realize that he'd been at it for hours and the night had advanced considerably toward morning. His eyes darted to the bed, where Ember stirred, rolling from her side onto her back.

Carefully, Nyte set the laptop on the floor beside him and stood up. His tail swayed behind him as he padded toward her, but his attention was on the sleeping female rather than his own body. He stared down at her from beside the bed.

Her arms were up, hands resting on the pillow to either side of her head with fingers slightly curled. A few strands of silver hair had escaped her bun, one of them resting over her cheek. Her face was serene, and as beautiful as ever. The blanket had shifted with her movement, its top now below her chest. He watched, transfixed, as the slow rise and fall of her breathing made the material of her nightgown draw taut over her breasts.

She looked so soft, so warm and inviting. So tantalizing. He needed but to slip beneath the covers and he'd be next to her with that voluptuous body against his.

He balled his fists at his sides, ignoring the bite of his claws into his palms.

I don't need that, however much I want it.

He was a nocturnus, an immortal demon of the night. He didn't *need* a mortal for anything. He could find happiness and fulfillment on his own.

Perhaps that was true. Perhaps he could. But those things had eluded him for centuries. Impossible as it seemed, he'd been entirely lost...even though he'd been right where he had trapped himself the entire time.

Yet as he gazed upon this witch, whose life would run its course in a blink of his eyes, he saw something ephemeral, made indescribably lovely and moving in its lack of permanence. There was a spark in his Ember like he'd not witnessed in any immortal creature, a passion more powerful and pure than any he'd encountered, paired with such kindness...

And it existed despite the loneliness she carried in her heart.

Delicately, he reached forward. The backs of his fingers brushed her forehead as he moved the loose strand of hair aside, guiding it behind her ear. Ember's mouth curled into the smallest of smiles, and something inside Nyte's chest thawed.

She wished for you, Nyte.

Foolish as he felt to even think it, perhaps some part of him wished for Ember in return.

Chapter Nine

Every day had been routine for Ember. She'd wake up, get ready, go to work at the boutique, come home, eat dinner and relax for a few hours, go to bed, and repeat the cycle. But these last four days, which had gone by faster than she'd ever thought possible, had been different. Because for the first time in a long while, she had someone to share those mundane moments with.

She had Nyte.

She'd grown up with her parents and two brothers in a house that had always felt lively and full. When she was twenty-two, she'd moved from Nebraska to Salem and had shared an apartment with Maggie. Their friendship had flourished, and they'd grown closer than Ember had ever expected from someone she'd met and befriended online. They'd chatted day and night, had watched tons of movies together, and had visited every bar, restaurant, museum, and tourist trap in town. Even during the quiet times, Ember had taken comfort in knowing that there was someone right there for her.

But when Maggie got engaged to Levi five years ago, she'd

moved in with him, and the apartment had been so silent, so empty, so...lonely. Despite Ember's years of dating and failed relationships, despite talking to Maggie and seeing her often, that loneliness had only grown.

Ember turned off the shower, opened the shower curtain, and grabbed a towel, briskly drying herself.

"And what did you do?" she muttered.

She'd bought a big, old house that felt even emptier than the apartment had.

Nyte had chased away that loneliness. Because of their tether, he was always near. Obviously, he wasn't here by choice, yet since the day after he was summoned, something in his demeanor had changed. He wasn't as grumpy and standoffish, and he seemed to have accepted their situation and was making the most of it. At least she thought so.

Since eating her spaghetti Bolognese, he'd taken to trying other foods. He liked pastries and hamburgers, and he had immensely enjoyed the dinners she'd cooked. Sweets seemed to be his favorite.

Ember grinned to herself as she rehung her towel, recalling the utter horror and betrayal that had been on his face when he'd taken his first sip of coffee. She couldn't blame him though. It'd been black, without any creamer or sweetener. Even Ember had shuddered, though she hadn't been able to contain her laughter.

She stepped into her underwear and drew it up her legs.

At the boutique, he'd often watched the people who came and went. There were times he'd stood so close to them that Ember was sure they must've felt his presence, but they always carried on as though he wasn't there. Other times, he'd eavesdrop on customers' conversations, and his animated expressions and offhand remarks often made Ember fight to hold in her laughter.

He thrived on gossip.

But it was her he seemed to watch the most. She would feel his gaze on her as surely as she would've felt his physical touch, and when she'd look up, those intense, cosmic eyes would meet hers, burning with the heat of a billion distant stars.

She'd felt that heat too. Every single time she looked at him, every single day, and every torturous night as she lay in bed, alone, with Nyte only feet away from her.

He'd even plagued her dreams, filling them with hazy, erotic visions of passionate kisses and sensual touches that left her achy and needy when she woke in the morning.

Ember grasped the sink and leaned forward, staring at herself in the mirror. Her cheeks were flushed from the shower, but that wasn't the only reason her skin felt so warm. A restless energy stirred inside her, a carnal desire that made her belly flutter and her clit throb with the need to be touched.

God, she should've masturbated in the shower while she had the chance to let off some of this steam. She wasn't sure how much longer she could go without some sort of release. Because fuck, Nyte really was the embodiment of her fantasy.

And he was right outside the bathroom door.

Ember blew out a slow breath to calm her raging libido.

You got this, Ember. Stay strong.

Because as much as she wanted Nyte, she wouldn't do anything without his consent.

Keeping her hair up in its messy bun, she grabbed the dark blue silk pajamas folded on the counter. She drew on the short, lace trimmed bottoms and pulled on the long-sleeved top, tying the three ribbon ties into bows at the front to close it. The silky material teased her skin with its caress, only making matters worse.

Ember groaned as her nipples hardened.

Shaking her head, she plucked up one of the face mask

packages from the tin holder and tore it open. She wasn't going to let her desire get in the way tonight. Her body would just... need to get over it.

Removing the mask, she held it up, watching her reflection as she lined up the eyeholes and mouth slit with her eyes and lips. As soon as the mask touched her, the cool gel soothed her heated face.

After smoothing out the mask, she grabbed another, removing it from the package as well, before opening the door, turning off the light, and stepping into her bedroom.

Nyte was lying on his stomach atop her bed with her laptop open in front of him. His wings were relaxed against his back, and his tail was draped over the side of the bed, the tip idly curling.

His position was so...human, which made it strangely charming.

"I hope you're ready for self-pampering night!" Ember announced, moving to the center of the room.

"Self-pampering?" He propped himself on one elbow and twisted to look at her. His eyes raked up her body, gleaming with familiar heat until they reached her face, when they flared wide in horror. "What in the hells is on your face?"

Before she could offer even a single word in response, he leapt off the bed and strode to her, leaning forward to study her face. "It has the look of a cursed object. The sort of thing meant to tear out a mortal's soul and use the husk of their body like a marionette."

Ember chuckled. "It's a hydrating face mask. There's nothing nefarious about it." She raised her hand, holding up the other mask between them. "And this one is for you."

His upper lip curled, and his nose wrinkled.

"Oh, come on, Nyte. Put it on!"

"I will not."

Ember stuck her bottom lip out and gave him the puppiest puppy dog eyes she could manage. "Pleeeeeease, Nyte. The last day of my work week is always self-pampering night, and since you're here, we can make a slumber party of it."

He stared at her blankly. "A slumber party. With a demon who doesn't sleep."

"You're staying at my place, so yes, whether you're sleeping or not, we're having a slumber party. It's usually when a bunch of friends get together, have a good time, and relax. So relax with me." She raised the mask toward him again, holding it up by the top so it hung in the air. In a singsong voice, she said, "It feels good on your skin."

"And what? When I peel it off, it will extract a sliver of my essence so you may use it to empower your magic?"

"Oh, don't be so dramatic. It just makes your skin feel soft and moisturized."

Tentatively, Nyte extended a finger, touching the mask with the tip of a claw to make it sway. He sneered and met Ember's gaze again, but his eyes softened as they held hers. He sighed like he was the most put-out being in all the universe and dipped his chin in a shallow nod. "Fine."

She squealed in excitement. "Yay!"

That sneer faltered, losing ground to the ghost of a smile. He waved to his face. "Put it on me, witch."

"Okay, hold still." She eased closer and raised the mask.

Without her asking, he crouched so he was more on her level, lifting one hand to sweep his dark hair back from his forehead.

Once she'd lined up the eyes, nose, and mouth holes, she placed the mask on, using her fingers to gently smooth the edges over his forehead, along the base of his horns, and along his cheeks and jaw. The entire time, his otherworldly eyes remained on her.

"There," she said with a smile as she ran her fingers over his chin a final time before stepping back. "How does it feel?"

He let go of his hair, allowing the black, curling locks to fall back into place. "Demeaning."

Ember chuckled and tapped the tip of his nose. "You look adorable. Now come on."

Taking his hand, she led him out of the bedroom and down the stairs to the living room. Once there, she released him to grab the thick blanket folded over the back of the sofa and spread it out on the floor. She tossed the pillows and back cushions on the floor next, kneeling to prop the latter against the front of the sofa.

Ember looked at Nyte over her shoulder, not missing that his eyes were unmistakably on her ass. That warmth stirred within her core once more.

It took everything inside her to not arch her back and lift her ass in the air like a cat in heat.

She cleared her throat, calling his eyes back to hers, and patted the blanket. "Come sit here."

The intensity in his stare did not diminish; not even the facial mask could lessen its impact. His shadowy wings grew wispier before dissipating like smoke carried away by a breeze, and he stepped to the spot she'd indicated, sitting down and leaning back against the cushion.

She smiled. "Comfy?"

"I am sitting on the floor, wearing this contemptuous second skin on my face, taking part in a *slumber party* at the whim of my dear little witch only because it pleases her. But yes, I am surprisingly comfortable."

My dear little witch.

Though Nyte had yet to call Ember by her name, the way he'd said those words sent a thrill through her.

It also made her heart thump harder to discover that he was doing this because it pleased her. He could have easily denied her, berated her for her foolishness, cursed her. But he was going along with this...because it made her happy.

"I'm...glad." Ember caught her bottom lip with her teeth to keep her smile from widening as her gaze flicked between his eyes. But as she took in his masked face, she couldn't stop a small laugh from escaping.

His eyebrows fell, scrunching the upper portion of the mask. "Are you laughing at my expense?"

"No, no. Of course not," she hurried to say as she braced a hand on the cushion and reached past him to retrieve the remote control from the end table. "Why would I laugh at you when I look just as ridiculous?"

Nyte snickered. "I suppose these are as far from flattering as one can get. And yet..."

She felt those otherworldly eyes on her again, blazing a path across the exposed skin of her upper chest and neck, right before she felt something else.

One of his claws hooked the uppermost ribbon of her top and tugged on it gently.

Ember's breath caught as she slowly sat back on her heels, her wide eyes meeting his.

The corner of his mouth was ever so slightly raised. "Is everything all right?"

Desire flooded Ember. Not even the mask could cool the warmth radiating from her. The way he was looking at her, the way his claw teased at the ribbon on her top, threatening to cut it away...

Her heart quickened, and her pussy clenched. Ember's

gaze dropped to Nyte's sensual mouth. He could rip that tie apart, could tear every scrap of clothing from her body, could do any depraved thing he wanted, if only he'd kiss her.

Nyte released the ribbon, moving his finger up to curl beneath her chin. The gentlest pressure notched her chin up, forcing her gaze to again meet his. "I asked you a question, witch."

Ember blinked.

A question? What quest—

It was only then that she realized how close she was to him. That her body had gravitated toward him, leaning in as though to do exactly what she longed to—kiss him.

Her eyes flared, and she jerked back. "Um... I, uh..." She pointed the remote at the television, switching it to a streaming service before quickly rising to her feet. "I'll be right back."

And with that, she made her escape to the kitchen.

It didn't help that she felt his eyes on her as she departed.

Ember moved her hands toward her flaming cheeks, meaning to cool them, but she caught herself before they could touch the mask. She settled on fanning her face instead.

"Get a hold of yourself, Ember," she whispered.

He was teasing her on purpose. Playing with her when he had no intention of following through with the wicked promise burning in his eyes.

What if Ember turned his game around on him? What if she teased him in return, made him desire her? Would he give in? Would he cast aside his notion of her being a lesser creature, of her being a silly, fragile mortal, and fuck her like she craved?

She drummed her fingers on the counter in thought before her gaze dropped to her chest. He'd been staring as she'd reached over him. She knew it.

Ember smirked. It would be a start.

Taking out a box of popcorn from the cupboard, she

popped one of the bags into the microwave. As it cooked, she grabbed her phone from the charger and placed an order for pizza delivery. Once the popcorn was done and had been poured into a large bowl, Ember took out a bottle of white wine from the fridge, along with two bottles of water. She grabbed a pair of wine glasses from the cabinet, tucked the bottles in her arm, and snatched up the bowl, carrying it all to the living room.

Nyte's gaze immediately fixed on her.

"What kind of movie do you want to watch?" Ember asked as she lowered herself onto the blanket beside him, setting the bowl of popcorn between them and handing him a bottle of water.

He accepted the bottle, placing it down next to himself. "I cannot pretend to know enough about movies to answer that."

Ember opened the wine and poured a glass. "We've watched a comedy and an action movie. I think you're ready for horror." She offered him the drink. "It's wine. Would you like to try it?"

As Nyte took the glass from Ember, his fingers brushed hers. That light touch left tingling warmth in its wake.

He raised the glass to his mouth, holding her gaze as his lips parted and he sipped the wine. Ember watched as his expression shifted. Curiosity became tentative appreciation, which faded swiftly, his features gradually tightening until the cords of his neck stood out. The expression was all the more comical due to the facial mask.

Ember chuckled.

Shuddering, he passed the glass back to her. "Do humans actually enjoy that, or do you take perverse pleasure in making yourselves suffer?"

With a grin, Ember swirled the golden liquid, making the

light dance upon it. "It's an acquired taste, and I actually really love it. It's perfect for unwinding after a long week."

She brought the glass to her mouth, making sure to place her lips in the exact same spot Nyte's had been as she took a drink. From the corner of her eye, she saw Nyte go still, and she heard his tail thumping the floor.

Ah, the tail. Always a giveaway.

Over the last several days, she'd noticed it swishing whenever he grew excited. But its boldest, most animated reactions were when he gazed upon her, often driving him to seize hold of it in exasperation when he thought she wasn't looking.

Ember set the wine down on the floor beside her and fanned herself with her hand. "It's feeling a little hot in here."

She took hold of the upper ribbon of her nightshirt and pulled until the bow came undone. It caused the already plunging neckline to display more of her cleavage, and she parted the collar wider still.

Nyte slammed his hand down atop his tail, pinning it to the floor, his eyes on her chest. "Feels...fine to me."

Ember smiled, plucked up a couple pieces of popcorn, and leaned toward Nyte, holding them up to his mouth. She knew this position caused her top to gape, knew that so much of her breasts was on display. "Try the popcorn. You'll like this better than the wine, I promise."

The muscles of his jaw ticked, and the faintest shudder rippled through him as the stars upon his skin brightened. He dragged his violet-blue gaze back up to hers. "Mayhap it is warmer than I realized."

She couldn't stop her smile from widening a little.

Though there was a hint of skepticism on his face, he opened his mouth. Something about seeing him like this, with that mask paired with those glowing eyes, those fangs and horns, was just as humorous as it was endearing.

Ember slipped the popcorn past his lips.

Nyte caught her wrist as his mouth closed around her fingers. Her eyes flared, and her breath hitched when his tongue laved her fingers, twirling around them to lick away every trace of salt.

She couldn't help but imagine that tongue licking another part of her, one that was currently aching with desire.

An appreciative hum rumbled from his chest as he drew back. "You were right, witch. I do like this better."

He released his hold, grabbed a handful of popcorn from the bowl, and turned his head toward the TV. "We're to watch a horror movie, then?"

Ember blinked at him.

What. The. Fuck?

Did he seriously turn this back around on me just like that?

With a soft huff, she leaned back against her cushion and muttered, "Cruel demon."

Well, considering he was an immortal who'd been around for eons, did she really expect that showing some cleavage would be enough to outplay him? The facial mask certainly didn't help.

And you thought you could seduce him while wearing it?

It was laughable.

Picking up the remote, Ember navigated to her watchlist and selected a thriller she'd wanted to watch for a while now.

They nibbled on popcorn and Ember sipped her wine as the movie played. The stakes and tension were part of what she loved about horror movies. She enjoyed the thrill of the unknown, the racing of her heart, the danger, the fear.

This movie definitely leaned into that building tension. It was psychological, the characters fueled by desperation and greed that clashed with basic human empathy. Such films always made Ember wonder how far real people would actually go if forced into similar situations.

She'd been so immersed that she hadn't even realized she'd gone through two glasses of wine.

Nyte voiced his thoughts and questions freely as the movie went on. With anyone else, that would've begun to annoy Ember. Not with him. There were moments when he was curious or confused, moments when he was appalled, but he was engaged throughout, and she was happy to have someone watching with her.

When it came to a particularly graphic, gory scene, Ember cringed, her hands shooting up to shield her eyes, but she stopped short of doing so.

"Why do you watch such movies if you can scarce stand to look?" Nyte asked.

Ember finally tore her attention from the screen to look at him, finding him studying her with his head tipped and his brow furrowed. "They're horrifying yet...thrilling. It's this strange feeling of wondering what it would feel like to be in their situation, to experience that fear, but being able to do so from a safe place. You get to look at terror and death and walk away feeling more alive."

"I suppose you humans have long found entertainment in death and bloodshed." He nodded toward the screen. "Are these mortals criminals offered up for execution, witnessed through your magic boxes rather than at town squares?"

"Are they criminals offered... Wait, you think what's happening in the movie is real?"

"Is it not?"

Ember gaped at him in horror. "No! Nothing that's happened in the movie is real. No one is actually hurt or dead." She pointed at her chest. "You thought I'd enjoy watching someone getting tortured and killed?"

"I've seen more public executions than I can count, witch. They were not attended by bloodthirsty monsters, but by unassuming humans. Laborers and tradesmen, aristocrats, families. Mothers and fathers with their children. People capable of love and compassion who still went to watch other humans die."

"Times have changed, Nyte. There haven't been public executions like that for a long time. Most people would be horrified if something like that took place. *I* would be."

Ember gestured at the television. "It's all acting and special effects. The actors are paid for their work, and they go home when it's done and continue on with their lives. Movies tell stories as much as books do. And just because we enjoy watching or reading about something doesn't mean we want to experience it for real."

Ember had consumed enough dark romance novels to know that for as thrilling as it was to read on the page, she sure as hell wouldn't tolerate any man treating her that way in real life.

Nyte frowned, eyes flicking over the screen. "Movies are... illusions?"

"In a sense, yes. It's all fake."

His attention shifted to Ember, his gaze heavy. "But the emotions are real."

She smiled. "That's the power of storytelling, especially combined with very talented actors."

Ember looked back at the movie just in time to get the biggest jump scare of the evening—unexpected pounding on her front door.

"Pizza's here!" she announced, pausing the movie and getting up. When Nyte began to stand, she waved him back down. "I'll get it. You can stay here."

"I'm disinclined to leave you alone, witch."

She chuckled as she walked backward toward the hallway,

wiggling her fingers in the air. "Do you think I'm going to cast a spell to make the pizza delivery person fall in love with me?"

He scowled. "No. But we have been watching a movie about humans being murdered in grisly fashion."

"Oh," Ember said a little uneasily as she dropped her hands. "Um...well... Murders at night in homes are not unheard of."

Nyte became a torrent of shadows, moving to stand before her so quickly that she instinctively jerked back from him.

His expression was deadly serious. "I'll accompany you then. Just in case."

Her heart quickened as she stared up at him with wide eyes. He was being protective of her, and damn if that wasn't sexy as hell.

Nyte raised his hands to her chest. His long, claw-tipped fingers deftly caught the dangling ribbons of her pajama top, which he drew fully closed, tying it securely. He motioned down the hall. "After you."

Though he'd tied the ribbon to conceal more of her cleavage, that didn't stop her nipples from hardening in response to his actions. The brush of his fingers, the teasing scrape of his claws, and the possessive gleam in his eyes stoked the embers of desire smoldering in her core.

I seriously need to do something about that if he won't.

Turning, Ember made her way toward the front door, and the trepidation she would have normally felt about opening it at this time of night was gone knowing that Nyte was guarding her.

Through the long, thin window next to the door, she caught sight of the red uniformed delivery man holding a pizza box in one hand.

Ember unlocked the door, opened it, and smiled. "Hello!"

The man's eyes widened, and he stared at her. "Um...got your, uh, pizza here."

Why was he—

The facial mask.

Ugh! How could I have forgotten that?

She chuckled awkwardly and waved to her face. "It's self-pampering night."

"Uh-huh," the delivery man said, his gaze dropping from her face to run over the rest of her.

"I'll gouge out his eyes if he doesn't raise them immediately," Nyte growled from behind her.

Ember grabbed the box from the delivery man. "Tip was already paid! *Thankyougoodnight!*"

She closed the door swiftly, locked it, and looked at Nyte, grinning. "One might think you were jealous."

He mimicked her grin, his fangs making the expression far more wicked. "And one would be incorrect."

"Mmhmm." She cast him a knowing look before she carried the pizza back to the living room.

She wasn't fooled one bit.

Lowering herself onto the blanket, she set the box down in front of her as Nyte returned to his spot. She reached up and peeled the mask of her face, folding it up and setting it aside, then beckoned Nyte closer. "Let me get that off you."

Planting a hand between them, he leaned toward Ember, the fire in his eyes accompanied by a hint of mirth. "Be gentle with me, witch."

"Aren't I always?" Smiling, she took hold of the mask at the base of his horns and slowly drew it away, revealing that exquisite, celestial face. She rubbed in some of the gel on the tip of his nose. "How does your face feel?"

He arched a brow. "Wet."

Ember laughed. "Your skin is positively sparkling."

"So it's exactly the same as it was before?"

Shaking her head, she set his folded-up mask atop her discarded one. "At least you'll never have to worry about aging. There's only so much we mortals can do to keep our skin looking youthful before the inevitable."

Something dark flickered across his features, chasing away the amusement that had been present in them. His gaze lingered on her before he moved it to the pizza box. "Let's have at it, then. I'm eager to learn whether this *pizza* tastes as good as it smells."

Chapter Ten

"You're fine, Maggie. Nobody's in the store right now, so I have a minute," Ember said, keeping her cellphone pressed between her ear and her shoulder as she neatly refolded and restacked the garments on the display table in front of her.

Nyte strolled along the clothing racks, absently brushing his fingers over the hanging clothes. His attention, as had become habit, was fixed upon Ember. His enchanting witch.

A smile spread across Ember's alluring lips. "Of course I'm free. You know I'm always down for Halloween shenanigans with you. Just text me the info, and I can grab the tickets if you want."

How could her smiles be so moving, so powerful, so tempting? They were genuine expressions of happiness, not attempts at being sultry and seductive. Yet those smiles pierced Nyte to his core. They warmed him from inside, and sparked tiny, fluttering sensations in his belly.

Ember's smiles were infectious. They made his lips twitch with the urge to curl upward, and very few of the customers who came into the boutique were able to keep straight faces when greeted by her smile.

"You don't have to do that!" Ember plucked up a handbag that someone had set in the wrong place and carried it to the proper shelf. "It's supposed to be my turn, Maggie. I don't mind if Levi joins us."

Nyte's eyebrows angled sharply down, and a scowl tugged at his mouth. "Levi?"

Ember chuckled as she wandered toward the jewelry. "He always makes the best costumes."

Clenching his teeth, Nyte followed her, but he couldn't quite make out what Maggie was saying through the cellphone even from immediately behind Ember.

She didn't seem to notice his nearness. All her focus was on her conversation with her friend.

With a growl, he dematerialized and reformed himself directly in front of her.

Ember gasped, stopping abruptly as her eyes widened. "Nyte!"

"Who is Levi?"

She lowered the cellphone to her stomach and pressed it there. "He's Maggie's husband." Smiling, she brushed aside the locks of hair that had fallen over Nyte's forehead, her fingertips grazing the base of his horn. "He's taken. Don't worry."

A calm settled over him at her touch, which soothed him even more than her words. He recalled one of the pictures in the box Ember had unpacked in her living room a couple days ago, when he'd helped her hang some of the images. Maggie's wedding picture. The man beside the bride must've been this Levi.

Ember returned the phone to her ear. "Sorry. A friend was asking about Levi." There was a pause as Maggie spoke before Ember chuckled. "Yes, it's a guy. Can you meet him? Uh..."

Her eyes flicked to Nyte's before she combed her fingers through her hair. "Maybe? He's pretty busy... Oh! He also usually works nights. What does he do? He, um... He's a bodyguard."

Ember squeezed her eyes shut and pinched the bridge of her nose as she grimaced.

My little witch is lying for me.

And it's adorable.

He grinned as he stepped away to lean his shoulder against the wall, watching Ember resume tidying the shop. Perhaps she wasn't quite lying; Nyte had been there to defend her from the dangerous pizza delivery man, after all. And he'd caught her when she'd fallen off a stepstool yesterday. Knowing how fragile mortals could be, he'd likely spared her serious injury.

His grin died as those thoughts reminded him of something she'd said during their slumber party four days ago.

There's only so much we mortals can do to keep our skin looking youthful before the inevitable.

Nyte was neither so foolish nor so disconnected from her kind to believe *the inevitable* referred to anything but death. His mind had returned to those words repeatedly in the time since she'd spoken them. For her, it had been an offhand remark, a mild jest.

But what she'd said had forced him to face a difficult truth. There would come a time—very soon by his perception—when Ember was simply...no more. The moon cycle for which he was bound to her was but a single drop of rain during a torrential storm. It would pass, and he would endure while she grew old and died.

And then he would exist in a world that no longer had Ember in it.

That shouldn't have bothered him. Mortals died every moment of every day. That was their lot, that was the natural terminus of their lives. But the thought of it happening to his witch left Nyte unsettled, left his chest tight and his heart frigid.

Despite everything, he was enjoying his time with her. He'd enjoyed the self-pampering night, enjoyed cooking and eating with her, enjoyed walking with her, talking with her, watching movies together, watching her sleep. He'd even taken pleasure in the quiet moments they'd spent together, when she'd read a book beside him while he continued learning about her world on the laptop.

He was enjoying...*everything* with her.

It seemed a heinous injustice that one day, she'd simply run out of time. That she'd be gone and beyond his reach.

The door opened, and raucous laughter filled the store as a group of five men entered. They appeared to be around the same age as Ember, and all of them were dressed in casual wear.

Nyte had seen many people of varied appearances visit this establishment. Ember had called them tourists—people who'd traveled to visit Salem, see the sights, and browse the shops. Most had been friendly, a few had been a bit careless in their handling of the goods but ultimately harmless, and only a couple had been rude. But there was something about these men and their demeanors that set Nyte on edge.

From what he'd seen over his long years of watching, human males, especially the younger ones, were more likely to be emboldened and antagonistic when they gathered in groups.

A blond man with a red hoodie picked up a handbag that was shaped like a coffin. "Yo, look at this!" He held it up and bared his flat teeth with a hiss, causing the others to laugh.

"This shit is so tacky," one of the other men said.

Rather than return the bag to its place, the blond man

tossed it onto one of the lower tables where bottles of perfume were on display, knocking them out of alignment.

"I have visitors, so I'll talk to you later, Maggie," Ember said, her eyes on the men. "Love you too. Bye bye."

She slipped her phone into her dress pocket and approached the group. For the first time, her smile seemed forced, belied by the wariness in her gaze. "Welcome to Darkly Romantic. Are you looking for anything in particular?"

The men turned their attention to her, and there was no mistaking the nature of the smiles that sprouted on their lips or of the gleams that entered their eyes. Fire ignited in Nyte's chest, its low, roiling, restless flames blazing a scorching path through his body. He gritted his teeth and clenched his fists.

"I think I am now," said the dark-haired man wearing a vest with a checkered shirt beneath.

"You got any underwear with bats or broomsticks or that kinda shit on it?" the red hoodie man asked.

"You asking if she has any in the store or if she's wearing it right now?"

They all burst into laughter.

Ember's smile disappeared. "We have some lingerie, but nothing like what you mentioned." She gestured toward the back of the store. "You can find them on the racks back there. We also have a men's section to the right."

"Mind showing us the lingerie, and which you'd recommend?" asked the blond man.

"My recommendation would depend on who you're buying for."

"Just...in general."

Her gaze flicked to Nyte's before she nodded. "This way."

She led them toward the back, and the men followed. With his eyes narrowed, Nyte stalked after them.

When she reached the lingerie section, she selected a black lace negligee and held it up for them. It had a bra-like top with flowing sheer fabric spilling from it like a robe. "This is a customer favorite. It's elegant and sensual."

A man with curly brown hair stroked his chin as he grinned at her. "Mind putting it on and modeling it for us?"

Nyte's claws bit into his palms, and the pain only intensified the blaze inside him.

Ember returned the lingerie to the rack calmly. "I'm not going to do that."

"Oh, come on." The man in the vest moved closer to Ember, fingering the lacey negligee as he stared at her. "How are we gonna know if we like it until we see it in action?"

"We have a fitting room. You're more than welcome to try it on so you can show your friends."

All the men laughed.

Curly Hair slapped his friend wearing the vest on the back. "How about it? You gonna model your junk for us?"

"Fuck no!"

The blond man chuckled and stepped up behind Ember, lightly running the backs of his fingers down her arm. "You got a curvy body and some big tits. I wanna see what it looks like on you."

Nyte bared his fangs.

The man had touched her. He'd touched Ember, Nyte's little witch.

Rage nearly compelled him to snuff out all the light within the shop and descend upon these disgusting mortal men, to reveal himself as a nocturnus in all his glory, fearsomeness, and ferocity. To gut and disembowel them.

But what would that mean for Ember? What would that mean for her shop? She'd said herself that beings like Nyte weren't supposed to exist in her world, and he didn't want to bring outside scrutiny upon her and her business.

Ember jerked away from the man with a scowl. Her eyes were hard, but Nyte detected a tremor in her voice when she said, "I need you all to leave right now, before I call the cops."

Nyte tasted something deeply troubling from her—fear.

The dark-haired man laughed. "You don't need to be such a bitch. Nothing wrong with some flirting."

The blond man lowered his head, petting her hair as he whispered in her ear. "I've always had a thing for goth chicks."

They closed in on her, and when she tried to push through them, they laughed and dragged her back.

Her blue eyes flared, sparking with terror. "Nyte!"

Fuck this.

For the first time in four hundred years, Nyte altered his form. His horns and wings vanished, the stars on his skin twinkled out, and his flesh lightened to a pale shade much closer to that of Ember's. It was a shape in which he'd often walked long, long ago. A human shape.

Shadows enwrapped him briefly, forming clothing over his body.

These men deserved more than simply being run off. They deserved to know fear. Tenfold the fear they'd elicited in Ember.

Magic flowed from Nyte. Gloom gathered along the walls, floor, and ceiling, and the overhead lights flickered and buzzed.

The mortals glanced up, a couple with concerned expressions.

Shadows erupted from the floor, engulfing Nyte and dragging him down. They swept him to Ember, and he emerged from their embrace beside his witch. She gasped when he curled his arm around her waist and tugged her snuggly against him, her body tense until he rasped, "I have you."

She looked at him, relief apparent in her eyes. "Nyte..."

He twisted, guiding her aside so he stood between Ember and her assailants.

The other human's heads swiveled toward him. They all jerked back, shocked by his sudden presence. The first hints of doubt wafted off them. That was always how it began; a tiny taste of what was to come.

"What the fuck?" one of them demanded.

"Where'd this asshole come from?" asked the man with curly hair.

The man in the vest snickered. "Bulk deal at Goths-R-Us"

"You should've listened to her," Nyte growled. "And you should not have touched her."

"Fuck off, cocksucker!" Curly Hair lunged at Nyte, thrusting his arms as though to shove him.

A pulse of raw power burst from Nyte, knocking back all five of the men before any hands could make contact with him. The nearest male stumbled and fell on his ass, and three of his companions staggered into clothing racks and display tables, knocking things askew.

The gathering shadows surged inward, swallowing the shop in utter darkness.

The blond man fumbled in the dark for a handhold by which to regain his balance, eyes wide and unseeing. But there was nothing for him to touch. "The fuck is this?"

"It's the same kind of gimmicky bullshit half the places in this town have," the dark-haired man said.

But belying his words, the uncertainty he emitted crept toward panic. His arms were out, swinging through empty air as though seeking out the clothing rack he'd struck only a moment before.

Ember wrapped her arms around Nyte, clutching him, and he tightened his hold on her. He willed himself to be seen—in the perception of these humans, he was a figure of even deeper darkness than that which surrounded them, with a pair of cold, distant stars burning in place of his eyes.

"Real funny," said the man with curly hair as he pushed himself up on fainty trembling arms. "Now turn the fucking lights back on."

"There is no light here." Nyte's voice swirled through the dark like an angry wind, striking at the men from all angles. "Only nothingness. Only the void."

The men jumped as they bumped into one another, grasping each other by arms and shirts.

"When we find you, asshole, we're going to beat the shi—"

Screams cut off the blond man's words as all five of them plummeted into the void, falling through that endless emptiness. Shadowy forms of inhuman, incomprehensible beasts rushed through the darkness, clawing at the men and snapping their gaping maws.

The men recoiled, contorting themselves and crashing into each other in their efforts to evade the creatures. They tumbled and spun, their cries rising and falling wildly, their panic only worsening their chaotic fall.

The terror radiating from the mortals was delirious, delicious, a feast like Nyte hadn't had in more than four hundred years. And it wasn't enough. After what they'd done to his Ember, it wasn't nearly enough.

But...it had to be. Because they weren't what was important.

In a flash, the darkness was gone, replaced by Ember's shop. The five men hung suspended in the air for a fraction of a moment before falling three feet to the floor, landing in a heap amidst the overturned racks and bumped-aside tables, causing merchandise to tumble off.

Once their disorientation broke, they scrambled to their feet.

"I'm getting the fuck out of here!" Red Hoodie cried.

"Yeah, fuck this shit," the one wearing the vest said, nearly tripping over his own feet as he rushed to the door.

All five men bolted from the store without looking back.

As soon as they were out of sight, Nyte turned his head to look at Ember. She was trembling against him. Cupping her cheek, he gently guided her face up toward his. He felt her tears against his skin right before he saw them in her eyes.

Something coiled around his heart and constricted, freezing everything inside him. Somehow, he forced words out of his mouth. "They're gone now. You're safe, my dear little witch."

Ember abruptly looked down, withdrew from him, and wiped at her eyes, careful of the makeup around them. "I know. I... Thank you. God, I probably look like a mess. I'm sorry. I can usually handle situations with guys like them, but there were too many of them and I..."

Her lower lip trembled as more tears filled her eyes. "I don't think I've ever been that scared before."

He'd sensed that fear, had tasted it. It had been sour and had left him hollow. He disliked her fear as much as he disliked her sorrow and anguish. And it had come upon her during the day, while the sun was bright and high in the sky.

Again, he reached for her face, this time catching her chin to draw her attention back to him. "It's all right. I wouldn't have let them hurt you."

Her eyes searched his. "But you won't always be here to—" She gasped. "Nyte, you...you're... Oh my God, Nyte, you're human!"

He scoffed. "Of course I'm not human. I just *appear* human."

With wide eyes, she pulled her face free, grasped his arms,

and stepped back to look him over, shaking her head. Then her hands were moving over him. She smoothed her palms over his shoulders and down his chest and abdomen, which he liked immensely, before taking one of his hands in hers. She traced her finger along his to its tip.

"Your claws are gone." She released his hand to wave above his head. "So are your horns."

Then she moved around him. "Your tail too!"

Nyte couldn't hold back a chuckle as he turned to face her. "None of it is gone. My form is simply...changed. I doubt the consequences of appearing before them in my true form would've been worth it. The last thing either of us wants is some would-be exorcist poking around your shop."

"What did you do to them? Because it's not like you're scary looking in...this form, but they looked terrified while they were floating all over the place. If they were to call an exorcist, it would be for that."

"I simply demonstrated what it would be like for them to fall through the endless void, detached from time and space, beset on all sides by nameless, faceless horrors."

"Why didn't I see any of it?"

He brushed a lingering teardrop from her cheek with his thumb. "Because I didn't want you to."

Ember smiled and pressed her cheek into his touch. "Thank you."

Fuck.

That smile and the way she looked at him with those luminous blue eyes would be his undoing.

Withdrawing his hand, he gestured down at himself. "So, what do you think?"

He'd fashioned his clothing after the garments she'd held up against him the first time he'd come to the store. It had seemed right in the moment, and that sense hadn't changed now.

She ran her gaze over him. A spark of heat chased away any lingering fear in her eyes. "I knew you'd look good dressed like that. And you are insanely hot in those clothes, but..."

He quirked a brow. "But?"

Meeting his eyes, she stepped closer and brushed her fingers across his brow, coaxing it to relax. "I love your true form more. I miss seeing your otherworldly eyes, your starlit skin, and your adorable wagging tail."

"It does not wag!"

Ember laughed. "It does."

He sighed, but his irritation proved both incredibly minor and immensely short lived. "I suppose if it is your preference..."

His magic rippled, returning him to his original form for her while keeping the clothes in place.

She gasped and quickly looked around the store, eyes halting on the entrance. "Can people still see you?"

Nyte's tail swung forward, its tip brushing her calf. "They'll see me, but they will perceive my human guise. You alone will see me as I am."

Something softened in Ember's gaze as she glanced down at his tail. "Really?"

"Really."

She grinned. "This changes everything!"

His eyebrows dropped low. "How so?"

"You can allow yourself to be seen as human. Meaning, we can go out and do things together, and you don't have to remain hidden while we're here."

Nyte frowned. "Mayhap I should reconsider this..."

"No way. No takebacks."

Shaking his head, he chuckled. "Let's close the shop and head back early, little witch."

"And now I'll have you to show off at my side." Ember slipped her hand into his, clasping his fingers. "I'll clean this up tomorrow. Let's go home."

As he closed his hand around hers, that word echoed in his mind.

Home.

He'd never wanted one as badly as he did right now.

Chapter Eleven

"Why must we go on this double date?" Nyte asked as they neared the entrance of the establishment, The Bubbly Cauldron Brewery. Its brick façade was lit by wall mounted electric lights that fought back the late evening darkness.

"Because I want you to meet Maggie and her husband." Ember touched his arm, drawing him to a halt. She stepped in front of him, smiling as she fixed the collar of his overcoat and straightened the lacing of the ruffled black shirt beneath.

Nyte gazed down at Ember. She wore a black top that was sheer above her breasts and along the sleeves, a long, layered purple skirt, a black belt adorned with a diamond crescent moon, and high heeled black boots. Her silver and black hair rested in soft curls around her shoulders and back. Black makeup framed her eyes, sweeping out in dramatic wings, and the violet, gray, and white shades of her eyeshadow made the color of her irises stand out beautifully.

But it was her dark violet lips that he couldn't look away from.

It had become increasingly difficult for Nyte to resist the urge to kiss her as of late, and this certainly wasn't making it any easier. She was so close, and her scent, more intoxicating than any aphrodisiac, filled his senses.

What would a taste hurt?

Nyte leaned forward, beckoned by those lips...

Ember patted his chest as she met his gaze, snapping him out of it. "Everything will be fine."

Drawing in a deep breath, he swung his eyes toward the brewery. "I still think this is a poor choice of meeting place. Humans are trouble enough, even without imbibing spirits."

Not for the first time, his thoughts returned to the men who'd invaded her shop two days ago. Anger crackled through his being at the memory. He could not deny that he'd been far more protective of her since that evening, keeping himself both visible and very near to her, eyeing every person who so much as looked her way.

"Lots of people meet in places like this." Flattening her hands on his chest, Ember leaned close, tipped her head back, and grinned. "I also plan to be one of those humans imbibing spirits. How much trouble do you think I can cause?"

He stared into her eyes. That grin, along with the sparkle in her gaze, did things to Nyte. They warmed parts of him that had never felt heat, made everything inside him feel oddly light and tingly. "A very great deal, witch."

"Then it's a good thing I have you to watch over me. Now, come on. They're already waiting inside." She slipped her hand into his and led him toward the entrance.

Whenever Ember took his hand like that, he seemed to lose the will to resist. It just felt so natural.

Damn it, why am I letting any of this happen?

But his feet moved, carrying him forward alongside her, and he made no effort to withdraw.

Long ago, he'd sometimes walked the night in human guise, yet he'd always done so as an uninvolved observer, rarely interacting with the mortals around him. Escorting Ember to and from the boutique for the last two days had been similar. He'd spoken to no one but her, and he'd largely watched his surroundings to protect her.

This was very different.

There would be questions, conversation, food and drink, unfamiliar social norms... It sounded exhausting. Far more trouble than it was worth.

No, that's wrong. It's not more trouble than it's worth.

Because he perfectly recalled the moment when Ember had first approached him about this double date. She'd been a little hesitant, and she had made it clear that he could deny her request, that he didn't owe her anything. The way her face had lit up when he'd tentatively agreed...

It was like every star in the night sky had come together into one impossibly radiant celestial visage.

The joy and excitement this brought Ember made it worth all the trouble. Nyte knew that should've alarmed him, should've made him question his state of mind, but again...

This simply felt right.

The moment they opened the doors of the establishment, music, voices, and the sounds of cutlery and dinnerware being used flowed over them. The same brick from outside the building formed the walls within, though it was broken by tall, recessed sections that were painted and decorated with large murals, the most prominent being a large black cauldron. A strange purple light shone on the mural, making the green liquid inside and the bubbles and steam rising from it glow preternaturally.

"Ember!" a woman called, immediately drawing Nyte's attention.

Maggie.

The woman smiled wide and waved.

Nyte recognized her from the pictures he'd seen. Her skin was pale, starkly white against her black makeup. She wore a form fitting black dress and silver cross necklace with a ruby at its center, and her long red hair hung loose around her shoulders.

The man who stood up from beside her was also familiar from a couple of the pictures. Levi. He too was clothed in black, from his zip-up jacket down to his jeans with tears at their knees and black boots. His beard and moustache were full but neatly trimmed, and some of his long, black hair was pulled back and tied at the back of his head. His mouth curved into a kind smile.

"Maggie!" Ember released Nyte's hand and rushed to meet her friend, practically bursting with excitement.

Nyte followed her path, though he did not match her pace, watching as the women took each other in a tight embrace, both of them bouncing on their feet and beaming as they did so.

In his experience, mortals and immortals alike were largely duplicitous, selfish creatures. They lied and plotted, they cheated, stole, and manipulated. They hid their motives behind false smiles. They all wanted something, and their dealings with other beings were conducted only to fulfill those wants.

Starling had been the exception. She'd never once asked for anything of Nyte, had never betrayed him, even if this latest stunt had initially felt like a betrayal. And though it should've been much too soon to tell, he knew Ember was the same. She was kind, loyal, considerate, and genuine.

As much as Nyte seemed unreal to her, she seemed impossible to him. This open joy, this blatant, honest display of affection and caring, he wanted to believe it couldn't be anything other than performative. And yet that wasn't the case. Ember and Maggie truly were *this* excited to see one another. The only thing either hoped to gain was the joy of the other's company.

Maggie drew back from Ember, her grin still wide. "I missed you so much."

Levi chuckled. "You two talk pretty much every day, my love."

"I know, but it's not the same as spending time in person." The red-haired woman stepped back and looked at Nyte. "And this is the guy friend you told me about?"

Ember moved to Nyte's side, slipping her arms around one of his. "He is. Maggie, Levi, this is Nyte."

Nyte could hear the smile in her voice, could hear the pride. And she'd introduced him from his side, holding him like they were in this together, like he wasn't a possession or a prize but an equal.

Maggie's smile softened. "It's wonderful to meet you."

Levi stepped forward and held out his hand. "Good to meet you, Nyte."

Before his recent consumption of modern human entertainment, this moment would've confused Nyte. He'd seen humans shake hands before his isolation, but never like this. A handshake was the sealing of a deal, a gesture to solidify an oath, something deeply meaningful and symbolic. He still wasn't sure how it had become a common greeting. But then there was a great deal about the world that he remained unsure about.

He clasped Levi's hand, mindful of his own strength. "A pleasure to meet you both."

"Come," Maggie said, gesturing to the enclosed table next to them. "Come sit."

Everyone sat, with Nyte beside Ember and Maggie and Levi across from them.

A waitress promptly arrived to hand out menus. "Hello!

Welcome to The Bubbly Cauldron. Can I get you some drinks? We've got a list of everything on tap in your menus, along with all our wines and cocktails."

Both Ember and Maggie ordered cocktails—whatever those were—and Levi requested a water.

"And you?" the waitress asked Nyte.

"Water for me as well, thank you."

When she left, Maggie folded her arms atop the table and grinned, looking between Nyte and Ember. "Okay, I've been saving all my questions for tonight. Tell me. How did you two meet?"

Ember chuckled, though there was a nervous quality to it. "Well, I guess it was...um..."

"She wished upon a star and summoned me," Nyte said.

With a quiet, startled squeak, she dropped her hand to his thigh in warning as her eyes widened.

Maggie laughed. "So what, did you just fall out of the sky or something?"

He smirked, patting Ember's hand. "Oh, there was no falling involved."

"He just appeared in the right place at the right time," Ember hurried to say as she looked back at Maggie.

"You know she's not going to quit without the details, Ember," Levi said with a grin.

Maggie nodded. "Time, place, what you were both doing."

Ember withdrew her hand and fidgeted in her seat. "Um, we were..."

"In her room," Nyte said. "She summoned me there."

"Oh." Maggie's eyes rounded, and she blinked slowly. "*Ohhhh*. Good for you, girl."

Levi chuckled.

Nyte could feel the warmth emanating from his witch as clearly as he could see it pinkening her cheeks.

Maggie tilted her head. "Was this after your date with Trent?"

"I met Nyte that night. He...kept me company." Cringing, Ember looked down and flipped open the menu.

"Well, whatever happened, it sounds like you both hit it off well enough," Levi said.

Grinning, Nyte brushed a finger along Ember's arm, enjoying the shiver that coursed through her. The way she reacted to his touch was entrancing. "We've had some fun."

Ember groaned. "Oh my God, all these innuendos are *not* intentional, I swear. We haven't had sex. Nyte's been rooming at my place and helping me at the store. He's..." She peeked up at him. "He's a friend."

A friend. Why did that word both thrill and disappoint him? Why did it leave him unfulfilled, wanting...more?

And she'd said it with a hint of yearning in her voice. Yearning he'd attempted to reject, but which had plagued him ever since he'd been summoned.

"How long do you plan to rent a room at Ember's?" Levi asked.

"We decided to give it a month and see how it goes," Ember said.

Maggie smiled. "You seemed to have gotten pretty close already, so it sounds like it's going well."

Ember met Nyte's gaze. "I've really enjoyed his company."

"And I yours." Nyte nearly added *my dear little witch* to those words, but that felt like something best kept between the two of them. Something her friends didn't need to overhear and question.

But she smiled as though she'd heard those unspoken words regardless.

The waitress returned with their drinks, setting them upon the table. Both Ember and Maggie's were bright and colorful, garnished with fruit and sugar crystals along the rims. After taking their food orders, the waitress walked off again.

Glancing up at him, Ember smiled. She picked up her drink, brought the rim to her lips, and drank.

Those fucking lips...

Levi leaned forward and propped his elbows on the table, clasping his hands as he directed his gaze to Nyte. "So, you been in Salem long?"

"No, I haven't." Nyte lifted his glass and sipped the water. "But there's something about this place that feels right. The..." His eyes shifted briefly to Ember. "Vibes."

Levi gave him a knowing smile. "I was visiting town for work during Halloween six years ago. That's when I first saw Maggie."

"Which is amazing consider how ridiculously crowded it gets here," Maggie said.

Slipping his arm around her waist, Levi drew her close. She leaned against him, rested her head on his shoulder, and cupped his jaw, stroking his beard with her thumb. A loving smile settled on her lips as she gazed up at him.

"One look at her, and I knew I couldn't stay away." Levi threaded his fingers through her hair. "My goddess who stole my heart."

For all his age and strength, it took a significant portion of Nyte's willpower to keep unease from creeping into his expression. That phrase—*stole my heart*—roused exactly the feelings he'd sought to escape during his time in seclusion.

Maggie hummed. "Can't steal what was freely given, my love."

Levi chuckled. "You're right. I pretty much handed it over on a silver platter, didn't I?"

"You did."

"And I've never seen a couple more in love than the two of you," Ember said with a smile. She looked at Nyte. "Levi rented an apartment in town a couple weeks after they met, just so he could be close. He wants to talk about stealing? He practically stole her from me."

Laughter bubbled from Maggie as she straightened. "He did."

"And I was left all alone. Allow me to drink away my sorrows." Ember brought her glass to her mouth and took a long drink.

"It's not like I up and disappeared!"

To Ember and her friends, this was undoubtedly warm banter. Their tones were light, their smiles wide, their affection for each other apparent. But Nyte couldn't hold back his heavy thoughts. Thoughts of hearts being stolen, of hearts being offered, of Ember being so alone.

"I miss you though," Maggie said more solemnly. "I miss our nights together, miss hanging out, just the two of us."

Ember set her glass down. "Me too. But I know we're both so busy with life, and you have Levi as part of yours."

Maggie reached across the table and covered Ember's hand. "I know you've had some horrible dating experiences, but you'll find someone who completes you the same way Levi does me."

Once more Ember's cheeks pinkened, and Nyte caught her glance his way.

She withdrew her hand from Maggie's and picked up her drink. "I don't know if anything could come close to what you and Levi have."

Nyte frowned, biting back the words that threatened to emerge from his mouth—the repudiation of her opinion, the acceptance of the challenge to prove her wrong, to show her that she deserved so much better than what she'd had thus far.

It would've been cruel to do so. Their current arrangement was both involuntary and temporary. He'd be gone in seventeen days...

And she'd be alone again.

Why did that thought produce a hollow ache in his chest?

He needed to steer the conversation away from such matters. He needed to prevent Ember from dipping into these moments of longing and sorrow.

Keeping up pretenses, Nyte took another sip of his water before setting the glass on the table. "Ember mentioned you make costumes, Levi."

The man's face lit up, and he nodded. "I do! I work in special effects makeup, prosthetics, and sculpting. I branched off and started my own business..."

Levi spoke passionately about his work and the costumes he crafted during his free time, with both Maggie and Ember adding little tidbits and offering him praise that he hesitantly and humbly accepted. Nyte found it engrossing, even though he didn't fully understand everything the man was talking about.

Part of that fascination was in humans as a whole. They invested so much thought, effort, talent, and artistry into making the fantastical seem real when it had always been all around them. He should've seen that as foolish, as another irrational human quirk, and yet... Amongst this company, seeing that twinkle in their eyes, it was almost endearing.

The conversation paused when the server returned to deliver their food, naturally picking up right where it had left off after Maggie and Ember ordered fresh drinks.

Nyte had seen many humans in such settings, sharing food, drink, and camaraderie, and he'd overheard many conversations. He would've been content to simply observe here, but the mortals continually involved him, asking questions to draw him in. It was refreshing in a way he hadn't expected. To be part of something he'd only watched from the outside...

But it was the attention from Ember that affected him most profoundly. Not just the way she smiled at him, but the little touches. The brush of her fingers on his forearm or shoulder, a gentle squeeze of his thigh, the fleeting glide of her foot against his. He craved more. Needed more.

Though he couldn't recall doing so consciously, he'd apparently shifted closer to her during the dinner, until their thighs were pressed together and her heat was radiating into him. Without his conscious thought, his tail curled around her calf.

Even when he realized what he'd done...he didn't withdraw from her.

More drinks arrived to replace Maggie and Ember's empty glasses.

"Oh, oh!" Maggie exclaimed. "Ember, do you remember the night you locked us out of the apartment?"

"Nooo," Ember groaned, turning her face and pressing it against Nyte's shoulder. "Don't remind me."

Nyte found himself suddenly despising his clothing. It was the only thing blocking her lips from his skin.

Levi grinned. "I need details."

Maggie giggled. "Ember woke me up in the middle of the night because she *swore* she heard noise outside."

Ember lifted her head. "I did hear something. So did you."

"I did. And what did we do?"

"We went out to investigate of course," Ember chuckled. "In our freaking nightgowns, in the dead of winter."

Nodding, Maggie took another drink from her glass before proceeding. "And our boots."

"Why didn't you call the police?" Levi asked.

Maggie pursed her lips to the side in thought. "I don't know. I don't remember."

Ember waved a hand nonchalantly. "Because when there's a noise outside at night, you have to go check on your animals and make sure they're safe."

"But we didn't have any animals."

Levi grinned. "You were in the city, Ember. Not back on the farm."

"It was instinct," Ember said. "Anyway! I grabbed a flashlight and the bat we kept by the front door, and Maggie..." She broke out into laughter. "Maggie wrapped one of her spike bracelets around her knuckles."

"Those things were over an inch long! It was a legit good weapon." Maggie held up her fist and threw an unsteady little jab.

Nyte chuckled.

Ember nodded. "It really was, because you bumped into me once with those and they *hurt*."

"I'm so sorry!" Maggie cried.

"It's okay."

"What happened next?" Nyte asked.

"Oh! So we went outside, in the snow, in our boots. Couldn't forget those. And I closed the door behind us."

Maggie snickered.

Ember pressed a finger to her lips. "Shhh! Not yet."

"Okay, okay!" The red-haired woman covered her mouth.

"So we were outside, and it was dark except for the streetlight, and deafeningly quiet. Until we heard it again."

"The crash was so loud."

"Did we scream?" Ember asked, brow pinched like she was straining to recall.

"I think we did."

"That's right! We did, because that's when we saw them."

"Them?" Levi asked.

Maggie hugged his arm. "The raccoons! There were so

many of them running around everywhere! And they left trash all over the parking lot."

"It was excusable because they were so cute," Ember said.

"They were, even though they scared the crap out of us. And once they scattered, we went back to our apartment... except we couldn't get in because Ember locked us out."

"The lock was wonky!"

"Our phones were inside, our keys were inside, and here we were, outside in our sexy, sexy nightgowns and boots in the dead of night."

Nyte had seen what Ember wore to bed, and he knew that she'd undoubtedly looked desirable that night. He wasn't sure there was anything she could wear that wouldn't be tantalizing.

Ember propped her elbow on the table and rested her chin on her palm, grinning. "We were pretty sexy, weren't we?"

Maggie waggled her eyebrows. "The neighbor thought so."

"He was like, sixty!"

"We were still sexy."

"You still are," Levi said, taking Maggie's hand and pressing his glass of water into it. "Drink this, my love."

"Mmm," she moaned as she did as he asked, and he helped her, tipping the glass as she drank deep.

Ember watched them with a soft smile.

Nyte didn't miss that expression, nor did he miss the flicker of yearning accompanying it. He knew jealousy wasn't warranted here. She longed not for Levi, but for someone to treat her with the same care and consideration.

Levi looked at Ember and Nyte. "I think it's time for us to head out. Maggie's had quite a bit to drink tonight, and I know she'll be regretting it tomorrow. It was nice to meet you, Nyte. Maybe we can all get together again another time." He glanced at Maggie with a tender smile. "Without alcohol."

Oddly, Nyte didn't dislike the suggestion. This had been

surprisingly enjoyable. Maggie and Levi seemed to be kind, warm people, and they'd readily accepted him. They'd made him feel like part of their little group, like they'd been his friends for as long as Starling had.

Nyte didn't intend to say the words aloud, but they came from his mouth anyway. "I would like that."

Chapter Twelve

Ember and Maggie stuck their lower lips out in exaggerated pouts as they looked at one another.

"I miss you already," Maggie said.

"I miss you too." Ember hadn't wanted this night to end. Seeing her friends, spending time with them, and laughing with them had been wonderful. She'd missed such carefree moments.

It had been even more special with Nyte sitting beside her.

He'd opened up with Levi and Maggie. There had been no animosity, no antagonism, no air of superiority. His smiles and laughter had come easily as he'd conversed with them, and Ember was sure he'd enjoyed himself as much as she had.

No one had suspected there was a demon in their midst.

But she'd known. She'd been hyperaware of Nyte all evening. The heat of his thigh against hers, the way his tail stroked her calf beneath her skirt, sending tingles through her, the wicked intensity in his eyes as he stared at her mouth, and the way he bit on his bottom lip with a fang. She'd noticed it all.

After they paid the check, Levi helped Maggie out of the booth.

She stumbled against him and wrapped her arms around his neck. "I love you so much."

Levi held her close. "And I love you. Now let's get you home."

Heart squeezing with a pang of longing, Ember subconsciously rubbed at her chest. She was in no way jealous of Maggie. She was and always had been happy that her friend had found a loving and adoring partner, but she couldn't deny that watching them hurt sometimes. They proved to her that love like that did exist.

But that didn't mean it existed for Ember.

Maggie waved as Levi guided her toward the exit. "Goodbye, lovely!"

Ember wiggled her fingers. "Bye!"

Nyte stood, straightened his coat, and offered a hand to Ember. "Shall we then, witch?"

Blinking, she looked at that gray, star-speckled hand with its long, claw-tipped fingers before slowly lifting her gaze to his. Nyte's cosmic irises were a pair of violet-blue stars blazing in the abyss, unwavering as they held her gaze.

Her heart thumped, and her belly fluttered.

Maybe it was her mind playing tricks on her, or maybe it was the alcohol, but she could've sworn there was a gleam of lust in his unearthly stare.

Smiling, she scooted toward him and slipped her hand into his. "Let's."

His fingers closed around hers, and with his aid, she rose, wobbling slightly. He didn't let go of her hand until she was steady enough to walk, and she noticed his hesitance before he withdrew.

When they stepped outside the restaurant, the wind was

blowing, carrying a chilly bite and the scent of rain. Ember's skirt whipped against her legs as they strolled along the sidewalk, and hair flew about her head in a tangle, making her laugh as she tried to pull the strands out of her face.

Nyte chuckled.

Ember peered up at him as she gathered her hair in one hand and held it to the side. "What?"

There was a small smile on his lips. "Maggie was right."

"About what?"

"You're lovely."

Warmth suffused her cheeks, chasing away some of the cold. She ducked her head and tried to hide her own smile.

They hadn't made it far before the first drops fell. It started in a sprinkle, a few sporadic raindrops here and there, but those were merely the heralds of the downpour that followed.

"Oh no!" Ember cried out as she threw her hands over her head in a vain attempt to shield herself.

As abruptly as it had begun, the rain stopped pelting her. Ember's brow furrowed. She could see sheets of water falling in front of her, hitting the ground hard enough to spray back up, but none of it was coming down on her. Just as oddly, the wind seemed to be flowing around her without touching her.

Slowly, she lowered her arms and looked up.

Ember's breath caught.

Nyte's wing was extended over her, shielding her from the storm. She could see the stars shining and twinkling amidst the shadows, could see the rain falling upon his wing from above, but not a drop broke through.

Reaching up, Ember brushed her fingertips against his wing. The shadows were as solid as his flesh.

His wing shuddered, and Nyte drew in a sharp breath, which was barely audible over the rain.

Touched by his thoughtfulness, she leaned toward his dark

form, clutching her hands together with a grin. "Awww, you do care!"

He glanced at her from the corner of his eye. "Silence, witch."

But the softness in the way he said those words shifted them from a command to a caress. An endearment.

Ember smiled, sidling closer to him as they walked. No one looked their way, so she could only assume he was keeping his wings hidden from other mortal eyes, but none of that mattered to her. All that mattered was Nyte.

She longed for him. She had since she'd first seen him. With each passing day, with each passing moment, with every new thing she learned about him, that longing had grown. Yes, there was lust, but this felt so much deeper. And it was getting considerably harder to hold back what she felt for him.

She didn't even want to think that in a little over two short weeks...he'd be gone.

The storm had only strengthened by the time they reached her house and stepped inside, and Ember fumbled in the dark along the wall for the light switch. When the lights came on, they were near blinding, causing her to flinch.

"Blazing hells, some warning please," Nyte growled.

"Sorry," Ember giggled, looking his way.

He stood with his eyes slitted and a hand raised to shield them from the light, his expression rather disgruntled. And she couldn't help but notice that he appeared to be completely dry. From the dark, unruly locks upon his head to his dashing attire, not a single drop of rain had deigned to land upon him.

Or he'd just...magicked them away.

Whereas Ember's boots and the hem of her skirt were soaked.

Holding the wall for balance, she tried to toe off her boots, but they were being particularly stubborn, with the side zippers keeping them firmly in place.

Stupid boots.

She took a step away from the wall, meaning to bend down and undo them, but the toe of her boot caught on her wet skirt, pitching her forward and tearing a gasp from her.

Though what happened next occurred in an instant, it felt like slow motion for Ember. Her stomach lurched with the certainty that she was about to faceplant, but the space in front of her darkened. Wisps of shadow licked at her, shadows she could *feel*, and the air thickened. Those shadows solidified. Rather than hitting the floor, she was halted by a solid body—Nyte's solid body—which had just materialized in her path.

She could feel his arms around her and his warmth seeping into her. Her fingers curled against his bare, star-speckled chest. His clothing was gone.

Slowly, she trailed her eyes up to meet his. He stared down at her, his brow creased as though in concern, the corners of his mouth curled down. His scent of woodsy incense and night air enveloped her, intoxicating her and stirring a fervid heat within her core.

Without thought, Ember rose on her toes and kissed him.

Her eyelids fluttered shut as her mouth lingered against his. She marveled at how his lips were so firm yet so pliable, and she didn't immediately register how tense Nyte had become, or the tightness of his hold on her.

He was as still as a statue, his lips unmoving beneath her own.

What have I done?

Ember abruptly pulled her face away and opened her eyes, a hot flush of embarrassment chasing away the fog of lust and returning her to lucidity. "I'm...I'm so sorry. I shouldn't ha—"

Fiery hunger glowed in his starlit eyes. He thrust his fingers into her hair, and his head swooped down as he dragged her mouth back to his in a hard, bruising kiss.

Ember's eyes flared in surprise, but they soon drifted shut, her body growing lax against his as she surrendered to his kiss. He groaned, clutching her hair, holding her head captive, not allowing her any escape. Not that she would have tried. She was exactly where she wanted to be.

In his arms, her body against his, with his mouth on hers.

When his tongue traced the seam of her mouth, she opened to it readily. It swept inside and curled around her own, claiming possession of it. The unexpected taste of him was a shock to her senses. It was like the crispest, sweetest water from an enchanted, starlight-bathed spring.

He tastes like heaven.

Pleasure swirled through her body, and a heavy pulse pounded between her thighs, deep in her core. Her hands slid up his chest and neck, fingers slipping into his soft hair.

Nyte angled her head, allowing him to kiss her deeper, harder. She moaned and returned it with equal fervor, unable to get enough of him, needing more. And he gave it, his tongue stroking and intimately dancing with her own. His kiss was hot and wet, sending a blaze through her, threatening to consume her.

But it wasn't enough. She needed him to touch her, needed this gnawing, hollow ache in her belly to be relieved. She needed him inside her.

Ember clung to him, body thrumming with desire. Each scrape of his sharp fangs on her lips sent a jolt straight to her clit, and all she could imagine was those fangs sinking into her flesh.

With a snarl, Nyte broke the kiss, leaving her immediately bereft. He pressed his forehead to hers, breath ragged and body trembling. His claws grazed her flesh as his hands tightened on her. "*Ember...*"

Her breath caught, and for a moment, her heart stopped.

He said my name.

And he'd said it in a way no one ever had—raw, guttural, overflowing with emotion and need.

Heart quickening, Ember lifted her head and sought his gaze. "Nyte..."

His expression was wrought with savage intensity as he banded his arm around her waist, pulling her body flush against his. "I fucking crave you."

Ember cradled his jaw. "Then have me."

His wings snapped out, spreading wide, before curling around Ember and cocooning her in darkness. But it wasn't total darkness, not by any means. Countless stars glimmered all around her, and their embrace was warm, solid, and thrilling.

And then the world fell away.

There was no floor beneath her feet, but somehow she wasn't falling. She was weightless and adrift with Nyte in this endless sea of stars, floating in nothingness, and she'd never felt so protected and secure.

When gravity reasserted itself, she realized she was lying on her back with Nyte propped over her. His wings dissipated, leaving behind tiny glittering motes that faded like dying sparks around her.

Rain pelted the glass of the window beside her, through which diffused light streamed to illuminate Nyte. And as her eyes adjusted to the new darkness, she recognized her surroundings. They were in her room, on her bed.

And she was completely naked. Her clothing seemed to have disappeared the same way Nyte's had.

The cool air settled over her, making her heated skin pebble.

A low growl rumbled from Nyte, and he lifted a hand to brush the back of a clawed finger over one of her nipples, making her shiver. He watched, rapt, as it hardened. Ember whimpered at the ache that touch produced.

"This beautiful body has haunted me." Nyte stroked her other nipple with the same gentleness, again staring as it responded to his ministrations.

Ember curled her fingers into the bedding on either side of her head to keep from reaching for him, afraid that he might stop. "You...wanted me?"

He chuckled, the sound low and dark, as his otherworldly gaze met hers, shining bright through the shadows coalescing around him. "Ah, my dear little witch, I have yearned to touch you. To wring every sound of pleasure from you, to see you writhe in ecstasy."

Those shadows flowed over Ember, trailing along her arms and legs, delicately caressing her skin and making her shiver anew. They swirled around her breasts and teased her nipples, and her breath hitched when she felt them slip between her thighs to brush over her pussy.

"Nyte," Ember whispered, shifting restlessly beneath him.

Slowly, Nyte eased back and sat on his heels, staring down at her. His eyes dragged over her body slowly, their leisurely movement completely at odds with the inferno of lust aflame within them.

He drew in a deep breath, chest swelling, and growled again. "Gods, how your scent has taunted me. Beckoning me to have a taste..."

Those wispy shadows grew more substantial as they coiled around her wrists and ankles like shackles. Nyte grinned, and the shadows binding her ankles pulled outward, splaying her legs wide and spreading her pussy to his hungry gaze.

Oh God...

Her sex clenched, and she felt her slick seeping from it.

"But I will have more than a simple taste, witch." Nyte curled his fingers around her inner thighs, pricking her skin with his claws as he guided them upward. "I will have all of you."

Chapter Thirteen

This was dangerous. Far more so than Nyte had realized.

The way Ember was looking at him now, with the lust in her eyes tempered by something soft, something affectionate, something...unfamiliar, it was nearly more than he could bear. It made him feel wanted. Full. Confused.

And it made his desire burn with the heat of a thousand stars.

Even at the height of his entanglement with Sarnessa, he'd not felt such want, such need.

His fingers flexed, and the tender flesh of her thighs yielded beneath them. Ember's cunt lay before him, pink and swollen, delicate and delectable, and the scent of her arousal...

Was this how mortals felt when they were drunk? This headiness, this haze, this absence of self-control? This yearning? Ember's sweet fragrance swirled around him, flooded him, permeated him, weaving with the very shadows that comprised his being, and he welcomed it.

His tail lashed, his body thrummed with anticipation, and the pressure low in his belly forced his cock to take shape. He couldn't withhold a groan. That flesh was so sensitive that even the touch of the cool air was almost too much to resist. He swore he could feel the heat radiating from Ember, washing over him in waves, enticing him and urging him closer.

Ember's essence glistened on her cunt like dew drops gathered on the petals of a flower. Nyte's hunger deepened and expanded, becoming something as vast and unfathomable as the empty space between the stars.

He couldn't wait any longer.

Dropping his head, he dragged his tongue up her slit, gathering every drop of her essence until he reached the hard bud of her clit. He gave it a flick. Ember gasped, her body jolting, but his shadows held her legs apart, keeping her from closing herself off to him.

"Nyte," she breathed, tugging at her wrist restraints.

His gaze met Ember's as her taste spread over his tongue. "Long had I heard mortals speak of ambrosia, of a drink so sweet and pure it is reserved only for the gods. Now I know it is no myth."

"Don't stop. Please."

He grinned as he moved his mouth back to her pussy, allowing his breath to whisper over her as he spoke. "Oh, I do not intend to, witch."

Nyte licked her again and again, his tongue caressing her labia, teasing her entrance, and circling her clit without applying direct pressure or contact. He relished her every reaction—the twitches coursing through her, the way she rolled her hips, every sigh and moan escaping her lips. All of it begged him for more without the need for words.

And though his desire had swelled to swallow up his entire being, though it ached with a ferocity like he'd never known, though he craved more than anything to be inside Ember, he obliged her. Her pleasure was his own, and her taste was a thrill in itself.

He needed more.

Pushing her thighs higher, spreading her sex wider, Nyte thrust his tongue deep inside her hot cunt. With his fangs pressed to her delicate flesh, he pumped his tongue. Her inner walls clenched around it.

"Oh fuck," she cried, arching her back. "Nyte..."

His cock twitched, and he closed his eyes in satisfaction at the sound of his name on her lips. Such passion, such reverence...

Nyte quickened his strokes, curling his tongue in a way that made Ember moan and strain against her bindings as she undulated her hips. He wanted to hear his name again, wanted to hear her crying it out like a benediction, wanted her to sing it into the night.

He directed his shadows to flow over her skin, to caress her, to enfold her in his dark embrace that he might feel all of her at once.

Her cunt wept with her essence, and he lapped it all up, thirsty for more. She was so sweet, so warm and wet.

She was...his.

Mine. Fucking mine.

Her breath came in shallow pants, and her thighs trembled beneath his palms.

Withdrawing his tongue, Nyte latch onto her clit and sucked.

"Nyte!" Ember cried out.

Willing the claws on two of his fingers shorter, he thrust them inside her as he lashed her clit mercilessly with his tongue. Her inner walls clamped around his fingers, squeezing so tight that the sensation jolted straight to his cock.

Hells, what would it feel like to be sheathed in her? To feel her body so hungrily gripping his shaft, drawing him deeper and deeper?

I will know soon enough.

Her hips moved in time with the pumping of his fingers, and he did not relent his hold of her clit.

Nyte lifted his gaze to look up along her body. Her eyes were closed, her cheeks were flushed, and her chest heaved with her rapid breaths. His shadows swirled around the hard buds of her nipples. Her moans escalated as the motion of her hips sped, urging him to drive his fingers harder and faster.

This sight of his Ember so swept up in passion, so lost in it, was the most beautiful, seductive thing he'd ever seen. The ache in his cock compounded, and he forced his hips down to press his shaft atop the bed. That added pressure did nothing to alleviate the pain; it only strengthened his need.

Her body tensed, and she let out a hitched, broken cry as liquid heat flooded her core, washing over his fingers and hand. With a growl, Nyte tore his lips from her clit and replaced his fingers with his mouth, once more thrusting his tongue inside her as he drank her essence. He circled her clit with his thumb, prolonging her orgasm and coaxing more of that delicious nectar from her.

When her cries faded, he didn't stop his ministrations. He gentled his touch and leisurely stroked her as his tongue laved her skin, licking up every drop. She moaned softly, her hips moving languidly with his touch.

"Nyte," she whispered, calling his gaze back up to her face. She was looking down at him, her eyes soft and gleaming with contentment. "Let me touch you."

"Soon, my witch." He brushed his lips over her inner thigh. It quivered, and he felt her pulse thrumming.

Mine. She is mine.

Before he knew what he was doing, his lips had peeled back, his mouth opened, and he sank his fangs into her flesh.

"Ah!" Ember gasped, her muscles tensing beneath his palms, but she could not break his unwavering grip as he drank the sweetness of her blood. "Nyte, what are you— Oh God!"

Her ragged breaths soon turned to cries of pleasure, and she trembled beneath him as she reached another climax.

When he withdrew his fangs, he licked the punctures he'd made, sealing the wounds but leaving his mark behind.

And that mark looked right there. It belonged there.

Nyte licked his lips to clean away the final traces of blood and essence smeared upon them before slowly crawling up her body, trailing his mouth over her as he went. He kissed her mons, her soft belly, and between her breasts, right over her fluttering heart. Ember wriggled, shivering with each touch of his lips.

When his pelvis connected with hers and his shaft nestled between the folds of her scalding cunt, a shudder wracked him, and he gritted his teeth against it. Pleasure buzzed along his spine all the way to the tip of his tail. He wasn't even inside her yet, but this was sublime.

Nyte sat up and caught her breasts in his hands, kneading their giving flesh. Hells, how could anything be so soft? Pinching her nipples, he gave each a teasing twist. She inhaled sharply and arched her back, grinding against his cock. The hot, slick friction against that sensitive flesh was nearly his end.

"My Ember, your body responds to me so beautifully," Nyte purred as he lowered his mouth to her breast, swirling his tongue around one of her budded nipples.

Moaning, Ember tugged against the shadow bindings. "Please let me go."

No!

That word burst from his very soul, resonating through him

with startling potency. It sparked an inferno in his chest, his heart flaring, raging, threatening to burst with a swell of emotion.

Now that he had her, he refused to let her go, refused to—

Her words from earlier struck him, piercing that emotion. *Let me touch you.*

Something rippled through him, something just as powerful as the possessiveness that had gripped him. It was his desire reasserting itself.

Had he not wondered over and over again how it would feel to have her hands upon his body? Touching, exploring, pleasuring... Had he not spent the darkest hours of these past nights fighting the urge to stare at her sleeping form and envision *everything* they could do, every way they could join?

"I will release you." Nyte dragged the tip of a fang over her nipple as he met her gaze. "But you remain mine, witch."

"Yes," she breathed, trembling. "I'm yours, Nyte."

Fuck.

Growling, he pulled her nipple into his mouth and sucked, wringing another moan from her. With a final, lingering caress, the shadows around her limbs dissipated, their magic flowing back into him.

As soon as she was released, her legs wrapped around his waist and her hands delved into his hair, clutching at the strands as she gripped the bases of his horns. The slight pain from those tugs only heightened his need.

Now. He needed to be inside her now.

Letting go of her nipple with a final nip of his fangs, Nyte pushed himself up, forcing her to let go of his head. Her hands fell to his shoulders and smoothed down his chest, where her fingers toyed with his nipples and their piercings.

Pleasure surged through him, making his cock throb insistently against her wet cunt. He bared his clenched teeth as he struggled to restrain himself.

The simplest of touches from her were nearly enough to undo him.

His gaze met hers. She stared up at him, her half-lidded eyes dark blue and smoldering, her hair a silver halo around her head. She was a vision of beauty in a way the immortal world could never match, every tiny imperfection only enhancing her loveliness.

Holding eye contact, he leaned over her, one hand propped on the bed as he wrapped the other around the base of his cock, aligning its head with her entrance. She caught lower lip with her teeth. Nyte didn't miss the way her gaze dipped toward the point where their bodies were about to connect.

By all the hells, that lustful anticipation was tantalizing.

But then her eyes flared. "You...you have *ridges*."

Nyte chuckled. "Mmm, the better to please you with, my dear little witch."

Slowly, he pushed into her. Her sex wrapped around his shaft, snug but welcoming, taking him inch by inch into her hot, wet depths.

Ember's lashes fluttered, and her lips parted with a shuddering breath, but she didn't look away from him as he pressed deeper.

A low growl rumbled from his chest. He slammed his hands down on the bed to either side of Ember's head, curling his claws into the bedding. He'd felt her from within with his tongue and fingers, had experienced her tightness, her heat, but it had been nothing compared to this. The feel of her clamped around his cock was at once maddening torture and rapturous bliss.

Nyte snapped his hips forward, thrusting into her until she'd taken every last bit of him. Ember's head tilted back, his name spilling from her lips. His grip on the bedding tightened as pleasure quaked through him, shaking his being to his very core, and his tail whipped around her ankle and coiled tight.

"Your cock feels so good inside me." Ember scoured her nails down his chest as she parted her thighs farther, taking him deeper.

Nyte shuddered. "And you, witch... You feel divine."

Her hands cradled his jaw, and even that touch sent a delightful flare of sensation through him. She pulled his head down until their mouths were a hairsbreadth apart. "Say my name."

He searched her eyes, seeking...what? Deception? Selfishness? Some reason to deny her? But as he stared, he found himself only more lost in her gaze, more lost in her. If the connection he felt to this mortal woman was a ploy, if it was a farce, he'd accept it just to experience these feelings a little longer.

Grazing his lips across hers, he rasped, "Ember."

He felt her smile before she closed her eyes and pressed her mouth to his. Groaning, he returned the kiss with a hunger that belied his outward calm. And she opened to him without hesitation, allowing him to deepen the kiss, to claim her mouth as fully as he was her body.

Banding his arms around her, Nyte rolled onto his back, taking her along until she sat astride him. She moaned as her body settled upon him, her sex clenching around his cock.

With a hiss, Nyte slid his hands to her hips and turned his mouth to her ear. "Ride me, witch."

She lifted her head and pushed the hair out of her face to meet his gaze, propping her hands on his chest.

He grinned and guided her pelvis, grinding her clit against his groin.

"Nyte," she moaned.

"Take your pleasure, Ember. Let me bear witness to it."

Pushing herself up, she sat back on him, causing his cock to sink deeper. His fingers flexed, and he resisted the urge to flip her over again and take his pleasure from her body himself. No... He wanted to see her.

Ember braced her knees on the bed and rose, allowing her cunt to drag along his shaft before she lowered herself back down, taking him slow and deep. Her head dropped back, and her eyes fluttered shut as she curled her nails into his chest. "Nyte, those ridges..."

He chuckled, though the sound was shaky in the face of the ecstasy created by her deliberate movements. "That's it, witch. Keep going." He bucked his pelvis upward, shoving into her and making her gasp. "Look at me."

She did as he commanded, her brow pinched with desperation.

"Good female." He summoned a wisp of shadow to swirl around her clit. "Look at me while you take my cock into that sweet cunt."

"Nyte..." Ember whimpered, but she didn't look away from him.

Her breath quickened as she continued moving up and down on his cock, guided by his grip on her hips. Each time her inner walls glided over his shaft, each time she took him into her hot body, pleasure spiraled through him, and the pressure in his core intensified.

Ember's need seemed equal to his own, for her pace soon became frantic even as the heat in her eyes grew. He matched her movements without thought, his body responding to her instinctively, feeling everything, watching everything.

Blasts of pleasure coursed through him each time she came down, making his limbs taut, followed by whispers of euphoria as she lifted up again. Every time she rose, he felt like she'd tear the very essence of his being out if she were to slide off him. Like he'd simply cease to be if their connection was severed.

Her body was a wonder to behold. The rosy color on her skin, the bouncing and swaying of her large breasts, the silver hair brushing over her shoulders, those gleaming blue eyes. He stared as her body took in his cock again and again, as his dark length disappeared inside her only to reappear, coated in her essence. Stared, ravenous, as her cunt stretched around him.

This was a taste of the paradise mortals thought they could attain after death. This was bliss given physical form, the peak of sensation, of intimacy.

And it wasn't enough.

Nyte wanted more, needed more. He wanted every part of Ember, to hold, to covet, to possess.

Every part.

Chapter Fourteen

Pleasure poured into Ember's veins like molten lava, threatening to consume her. It coiled in her belly, winding tighter and tighter, thrumming with every stroke of Nyte's ridged cock inside her and every teasing swirl of the shadows circling her clit. And despite the burning in her thighs, she couldn't stop.

"Come for me, witch," Nyte growled, his claws biting into her flesh.

It should've hurt. She felt the warm trickle of blood where he'd broken her skin, but the pain only amplified the pleasure, reminding her of his teeth sinking into her thigh and the ecstasy that had followed.

This wasn't normal for Ember. But nothing with Nyte was normal, was it? He was a demon, a literal creature of the night, a being who was supposed to be nothing more than myth. He was her wish and her fantasies incarnate.

So who the fuck cared about normal? She didn't need it.

Because in this moment, he was hers.

And as Ember held his gaze and basked in the reverence shining in his eyes, she knew she was his too, if only for this little while.

Her breath came in shallow pants, and her body trembled with the need to come. She teetered on the precipice, and she felt the end nearing with every stroke of his cock.

Another wisp of shadow trailed up her arm, cool and light upon her skin, before it cradled and caressed her cheek. She turned her face toward it, but still didn't look away from him, his command holding strong.

"Give yourself to me, Ember," Nyte coaxed in a deep, husky voice.

Unable to withstand it any longer, she fell forward, bracing her hands to either side of his head as she continued to move upon him. Her hair fell in a curtain around them, and their ragged breaths mingled.

Nyte's hands slid from her hips to her ass, clutching her cheeks and spreading them wide as he thrust into her. "Say you are mine."

The altered angle allowed his ridges to strike a new spot within her and made her clit grind against his pelvis. It was all she needed. Rapture cleaved through Ember. Her lips parted in a silent scream, and her movements faltered as her body went taut and her sex contracted.

Nyte immediately took control, planting his feet on the bed as he pounded up into her pussy, each stroke harder and faster than the last. That relentless pace only intensified her pleasure, prolonging her orgasm.

"Say it!" he commanded, his features turning savage.

Breath coming in short, surrendering moans, she cried, "Yours! I'm yours."

He slowed his thrusts, and that was when she felt it—the cool touch of his shadows prodding at the entrance of her ass.

Ember gasped as the shadows slipped inside. "Nyte, what... What are you doing?"

He flicked his tongue over her bottom lip. "Claiming every part of you, witch."

The shadows in her ass solidified, growing larger and thicker, expanding her. The sensation was so foreign, so odd, and so fucking good. As the shadow pumped in and out of her in time with the thrusts of his cock, she felt ridges forming upon it.

Is that... It can't be.

But she knew it was. A second cock, formed out of darkness.

Ember gripped the bedding at the thrilling feeling. Despite having no lubrication, there was no pain, only the brief burn of him stretching her. It felt...unreal, gliding impossibly smoothly, yet that shaft was as real and solid as the first.

She'd never felt so full in her life, and this... Oh God, this was almost too much. Each stroke of those cocks spread long, pulsing waves of pleasure through her, making her skin tingle. A maelstrom of sensation grew inside her, and she yielded to it. To him.

"We fit together so perfectly," Nyte rasped before capturing her mouth in a searing kiss.

That heat grew, and as though fueled by it, he pumped his hips faster, resuming the frantic pace he'd kept moments before. Swallowing her needy moans, Nyte drove his cocks into her aching pussy and untried ass, each pummel sending white-hot blasts of pleasure through Ember.

Everything narrowed down to feeling. The feel of his claws, the feel of his body, the feel of his insatiable kiss and of those cocks stretching her, filling her, their ridges hitting every sensitive spot inside her.

Her body wasn't her own. She'd given it over to him utterly.

When those flames consumed her, she surrendered to the scalding sweetness of ecstasy. Her body locked up, her pussy and ass clenching around his cocks as liquid heat poured from her.

Nyte snarled. Shadows flowed from him, enveloping both his body and Ember's, and once again the world vanished. Reality snapped into place with their positions reversed—Ember on her back and Nyte looming over her, his hips slamming between her thighs without cease.

His wings spread, shrouding the surrounding room with swaths of the night sky, and the stars on his skin flared. His hands clutched at her hips, fingers bruising, claws pricking, pulling her toward him forcefully to meet his every thrust.

Tension seized his body, and his lips peeled back to reveal his fangs. "You are *mine*."

With a brutal growl, he drove into her again as deep as he could possibly go, and it stole her breath. His cocks swelled within her. She grasped his arms, digging her nails into his flesh as he threw his head back and came with a roar, his eyes squeezing shut.

Heat erupted from his shafts, flooding her and launching her into the heavens with another climax.

But she didn't let her eyes close. She fought to keep them open, to stare up at him as pleasure swept him up. His gray skin darkened to match the black of his limbs, making those stars glare like countless supernovas in the endlessness of space. The light from his eyes was so intense that it leaked through his eyelids. Strands of black, wavy hair dangled in his otherworldly face.

He was beautiful. An inhuman creature who should've seemed so cold, so distant, so dark, and yet he shone with a radiance so profound and alluring that Ember couldn't look away from him. She didn't want to look away.

And never had that radiance been as pure as it was right now, as they rode out these waves of mutual rapture.

Chapter Fifteen

Galaxies swirled and collided behind Nyte's eyelids as pleasure coursed through him like waves of light racing across the cosmos. Never had he been so aware of his physical form, never had he been so overwhelmed by sensation. He felt heavy, lethargic, but sated.

If this ecstasy was the chains binding him to this flesh, to this mortal realm, he could muster neither the strength nor the willpower to shed them.

He collapsed forward, catching himself on his hands over Ember. Ragged breaths tore in and out of his throat. His arms trembled, and his cocks twitched with jolts of pleasure at every miniscule movement of her body.

The starlight behind his eyelids became decidedly warmer when Ember's hands brushed up his chest. He smiled as her fingers stroked along his neck and traced his jaw, her touch so soft, soothing, and affectionate that he feared he would be lulled into losing hold of his current form if it continued.

By all the hells, fucking her had been rapturous, but these leisurely, tender caresses were something else entirely.

Her legs slid down from his waist, coming to rest atop the bed, and her body relaxed beneath him. Her hands slowed, their touch gentling further. She hummed. It was such a quiet, content sound. Nyte couldn't help but feel a swell of pride and satisfaction at hearing it.

Too soon, Ember's hands fell away, and she lay languid beneath him.

He could've eased himself down and lain with her, could've relished this intimacy, this stillness, after all that frantic motion. Instead, he opened his eyes and looked down at his witch. Her eyes were shut, her dark lashes resting upon flushed cheeks, and her brow was smooth. Those full lips were ever so slightly parted, and her breaths were deep and even.

She was asleep. Soundly, peacefully asleep, not just in his presence but with him atop her.

With him inside her.

Nyte stilled. Cold crept through him in the wake of another echo of pleasure, and ice formed around his heart.

What had they done?

What have I done?

He pushed himself up on his knees, gritting his teeth against the torturous friction the movement created between their bodies.

Thoughts careered through his mind, quick and chaotic as a meteor shower lighting up the night sky. Carefully, he sat back, slowly pulling his cocks free from Ember.

It was all he could do to suppress a growl at that drag of flesh against flesh. Even in her sleep, her body seemed reluctant to relinquish its hold on him.

He knew better than to look, but his eyes dipped regardless. The delicate pink flesh of her cunt and ass glistened as his cum seeped from them, the glittering motes within it shining silver in the dim light. More silvery flecks were spread on her inner thighs and ass cheeks.

A powerful, primal urge rose inside him to press his essence back into her, to ensure none escaped. Though no child could be conceived between them, he felt an instinctual drive to keep part of himself inside her, to mark her even from within.

His hand had already moved halfway toward her sex before he caught himself.

Sunlight scorch him to cinders, had he learned *nothing*?

With a beat of his wings, he dissipated to shadow and reformed himself away from the bed. Away from Ember, from this witch, this...this temptress.

Nyte paced about the bedroom, finding little comfort in the darkness and less still in his thoughts. His tail lashed erratically.

All that denial, all that determination, all that resistance, and he'd succumbed anyway. He'd given in to lust. Had let his desire to kiss her, to touch her, to rut her, become a driving need that refused to be ignored. Even now he felt that pull toward her, and he could no longer pretend it was merely an effect of the binding spell.

No, this was of a vastly different and far more troubling nature.

What he and Ember just shared had been unlike anything he'd had with Sarnessa. This... This had shattered his soul into countless pieces and reassembled them with fragments of Ember mixed in. It had been so much more than sex, so much more than sensation.

He wasn't just yearning, he was *feeling*.

And that was...unsettling. Deeply, deeply unsettling.

Unbidden, his hand rose to rub at his chest. Phantom pain radiated from his heart, ghostly whispers of soul-crushing agony, overshadowed by a much deeper pain that had been seared into his being.

Curling his fingers so his claws raked his flesh, he halted.

He was standing before Ember's bed, his eyes already falling to behold her.

She lay naked atop the bedding, one arm bent so her hand rested near her head. She'd turned her face toward him, and her soft breaths made the hair spread beside it sway gently.

Nyte couldn't stop his gaze from roaming over her. Her nipples remained pert, darkened by his attentions, and there was dried blood on her hips where his claws had scratched her. All that pale, supple flesh, all those generous curves... Her body begged for the touch of his hands, of his mouth.

His eyes fixated lower, where his cum glittered on her inner thighs and bare cunt.

He gritted his teeth. His cocks strained toward her, stiff enough to hurt. He could feel the blend of her slick and his essence drying on his shafts, could smell their combined fragrance on the air, could still taste her sweet release on his tongue.

Nyte's skin tingled. That tingling rapidly became a thrum that permeated him. It felt as though his entire being was desperately seeking her out, as though all the shadowy magic that comprised him needed to be with her *now*.

Despite his unease and inner turmoil, he was sorely tempted to climb onto Ember's bed, wedge himself between her thighs, and slide back into her delicious heat. While their bodies were intertwined, he didn't have to think, didn't have to worry, didn't have to do anything but feel pleasure beyond his wildest imaginings.

For all his years, for all the knowledge and language he'd absorbed, he had no words to adequately describe what he and Ember had shared.

That only made all of this more alarming.

Whatever else this was, it was a weakness. And he'd vowed never to be left so vulnerable again.

Magic rippled through the air behind Nyte in a familiar signature.

Instinctively, he wove a blanket of shadow, willing it into shape from the ether and draping it over Ember's slumbering form, covering her nakedness from her upper chest down.

She stirred only to turn her head slightly with a gentle sigh.

"So thoughtful of you," Starling said from over Nyte's shoulder.

He grunted. There'd been only one thought behind the gesture.

None may gaze upon my Ember's form but me.

Hells, he wanted to possess her, body and soul. Wanted her to be his in every way. But he feared that this little witch had already claimed possession of him.

Nyte forced his cocks to dissipate, unable but to mourn the loss of the essence that had clung to them.

Starling landed upon his shoulder, and her soft glow fell upon Ember to make that tousled silver hair shimmer. The sprite bounced in place. "Ooo! She looks like a woman who has been quite thoroughly satisfied."

Clenching his jaw, Nyte turned and stalked away from the bed, taking Starling with him. Voice low, he said, "That is no concern of yours."

Giggling, Starling plopped into a sitting position, swinging her legs to kick him with her tiny heels in a quick rhythm. "What of you, Nyte? Have you been thoroughly satisfied as well?"

No. Never. I need more of her, more, more, more!

"Do I sound satisfied?" he grated as he glided down the stairs.

"You sound grumpy, just as ever. But you rarely sound how you feel. Did you not enjoy your witchling?"

Enjoy? I was utterly shattered.

"Whatever you hope will happen here, sprite, it shall not. There is nothing between myself and the witch." An ache tore through his chest, nearly making him flinch; the sensation was fire and ice all at once, burning and freezing. "And it shall remain so until your accursed spell has run its course."

Starling darted off his shoulder and hovered before him, both sets of arms folded across her chest. Her three eyes narrowed in a glare. "You will not convince yourself with such words."

He halted, eyebrows angling down toward his nose. "I'm not trying to convince myself, Starling."

She impatiently waved a hand.

Nyte balled his fists at his sides. Tumultuous emotions roiled inside him, more volatile than a collapsing star. Energy blazed through him, but it left him feeling unsteady and off rather than invigorated.

His throat was tight when he finally spoke. "I'll not risk suffering that again."

Frowning, the sprite lowered her arms and tilted her head. "So you will just hide instead? Blessed with eternity and determined to waste it away?"

Nyte closed his eyes and drew in a deep breath. He couldn't ignore the traces of Ember's scent perfuming the air, however much easier it would've made his life at that moment. "I've no wish to fight."

"Yet it seems you must. With yourself."

He shook his head. "Again you—"

"Hush, demon. You are so near to something wonderful, and *you* are ever the obstacle barring your path. You have a great deal to ponder, Nyte. Do not flee from it."

"Damn it, Starling." He opened his eyes, but the sprite was already gone. She always ensured she had the last word, with no consideration for how infuriating that was for him.

His tail whipped the air as he twisted to glance up toward the top of the stairs. That ache persisted in his chest, even more raw and potent than before, and he massaged it distractedly.

There was nothing to contemplate, nothing to consider. The only thing he was drawing near to was the next full moon and the end of this summoning.

All he'd shared with Ember was...sex. Nothing more. And that was all it would remain. They'd granted one another mutual release, and they would not do so again. A couple more weeks of resolve and he'd be free...

He would not again submit to temptation, would not open himself to the potential pain.

Not when so much of it lingered in him after four centuries.

Chapter Sixteen

The sweetest of dreams faded away as Ember woke up to the sound of rain. Her lashes fluttered open. The morning sky outside her window was overcast, gloomy with dark clouds, and the rainwater streamed down the glass panes in rivulets.

She smiled.

What she'd experienced last night hadn't been a dream. She recalled every kiss, every touch, every word that had been spoken. Recalled the feel of Nyte beneath her, over her, inside her, recalled the light in his eyes and the brilliant shine of the stars on his skin.

But most of all, Ember recalled the intense, bestial way in which he'd fucked her.

Her skin tingled and her core clenched with the memory. He'd possessed her body, mastered it, had laid claim to it, but it was the demand he'd made of her that had held the most dangerous, tempting promise of something more. Of something deeper, something profound.

Say you are mine.

It had been more than she'd dared hope for.

With a soft moan, Ember closed her eyes, rolled onto her back, and stretched, the blanket sliding down her breasts and brushing over her sensitive nipples. Her body was sore, and she could feel the stings of the small wounds Nyte had left behind with his teeth and claws, but she loved it. It was further proof of what they'd shared. Most prominent of all was the sensation in her pussy and ass. Both were tender with echoes of the pleasure his cocks had wrought.

God, but Ember wanted him again.

Today was her day off, and she was in absolutely no rush. She wanted to relish this moment and all the delightful aches and pains that had come from a night of euphoria.

Ember brushed her hand over the mattress beside her, seeking Nyte, but she found only unoccupied bedding that was cool to the touch. Turning her head, she opened her eyes. She was indeed alone on the bed.

That he wasn't there with his arms around her, holding her while she slept, sent a pang through her chest and sapped some of her joy. But that was ridiculous. Nyte didn't sleep. She couldn't expect him to lie with her all night, bored out of his mind.

Yet that knowledge didn't diminish her disappointment and the accompanying loneliness.

Ember sat up and blinked. It wasn't her blanket draped over her, but one formed of shadow. Had Nyte done this after she'd fallen asleep?

It's pretty obvious, Ember. Who else can summon and shape shadows?

Her lips curled into a smile. She could almost feel the phantom touches of his shadows like they were still moving over her body, stroking her intimately and binding her. But this? Covering her with a blanket made of those very shadows to shield her and keep her warm as she slept? It was incredibly thoughtful and sweet.

She picked up the shadow blanket, moving it aside as she shifted her legs and scooted to sit on the edge of the bed. Her breath hitched. Warm liquid seeped from her pussy.

Ember looked down. The bitemark left by his fangs and the bruising around it were stark against her skin, but that wasn't what caught her attention. Sparkling silver glitter was smeared all over her inner thighs. She reached between them, dragged a finger through her sex, and raised her hand. Thick, glittery cum coated it. Her brows shot upward.

Well...that makes sense. He is a night demon, after all. Why wouldn't he have stardust in his jizz?

She glanced at the bedding. The dim morning light shone upon it, revealing more sparkling evidence of what they'd done last night. She wiped her finger over the blanket.

Her first day off was usually laundry day, anyway.

Turning her face back toward the room, she sought out her demon. "Nyte?"

She spotted him in the most obvious place—the far corner of the bedroom, well outside the reach of the daylight, sitting with his back to the wall and a cloud of shadows around him. The darkness was thick enough that she could barely see the stars on his skin. Only his eyes were clear.

Smiling, Ember braced her hands on the bed and leaned forward. "Why don't you come back to bed?"

Nyte's eyes shifted to her. There was a coldness in them, icier than anything she'd seen since the night she'd summoned him. "No."

His rejection hurt, but she didn't let it deter her. Whatever had set him off and put him in this broody mood, she would help him overcome it.

She lifted her hand, and using the same finger she'd

touched herself with—which was now sparkling with his cum—she brushed her bottom lip. His scent filled her nose. In a playful tone, she said, "If you come here, I'll suck you off."

On a whim, she slipped her finger into her mouth. His flavor spread on her tongue as she slowly pulled her finger free. It was like tasting the sweetest rain.

Nyte's eyes flared and brightened briefly, and the shadows around him seemed to darken afterward. But he remained otherwise still, offering no reply.

Ember frowned. What had changed between last night and this morning?

Rising from the bed, she padded across the room. The air was cool on her naked skin as she neared her demon.

"Nyte?" She reached out to touch his bent knee, but before her fingers made contact, he disappeared, the shadows that had surrounded him blinking out of existence.

She whirled to find him standing in the center of the room with his arms folded across his chest, his shoulders squared, and his chin raised.

"Enough, witch."

"Nyte, what the hell is going on? Everything last night was...was perfect. Why are you putting this distance between us like what we did didn't mean anything?"

"Because it didn't."

Ember flinched, stricken by his words. "What?"

His jaw ticked. "It cannot happen again. Will not."

Feeling suddenly vulnerable in her nakedness, she wrapped her arms around herself. It was like her chest was caving in, constricting her insides, making it hard to breathe. They'd given themselves to one another. He'd called her his. "Why are you saying these things? Why are you doing this?"

Nostrils flaring, he turned his face away. His already stiff posture tensed further, and she saw his claws biting into his biceps, saw his wings draw tight against his back, saw his tail lash down toward the floor.

The silence in the bedroom was stifling, a suffocating miasma dominating the air, making it only more difficult for Ember to fill her lungs. Her eyes burned with the threat of tears. This was it? After all the time they'd spent together, after one of the best nights of her life, he was just going to leave her with all this hurt and not a single answer, not a glimmer of insight?

Not a single reason?

She couldn't be in here with him like this, couldn't stand it. The pain was too raw, the silence too loud, and if she was going to break down and cry, she didn't want him to witness it.

As she stepped toward the bathroom to leave, Nyte spoke. His voice was thick and low, as though he were fighting to force out words that had no desire to be uttered. "I was involved with another female, long ago. A succubus named Sarnessa."

Ember froze. Confused waves, at once hot and cold, coursed over her skin, making it crawl. A succubus? She turned her eyes back toward him, frowning.

Nyte lowered his chin, fixing his gaze on the floor. "Though I had observed humanity for millennia before I encountered her, I remained naïve regarding many things. I'd seen so much, but I had experienced so little. I'd witnessed love and lust but had never felt it, had watched sex but had never partaken. I'd had no such emotions, no such desires. I was intimate with human fear, but...not with intimacy itself.

"I first saw her while she was fucking a hapless mortal. She exhibited such unbridled passion, such...life. I was entranced. Of course, she was feeding from him. Drained him nearly to death. And as she stepped away from her victim, smiling, satisfied, and glowing, she noticed me. And her smile grew." The faintest tremor ran through his wings. "I was taken by her immediately. She exuded what I'd only observed before then... desire, lust, and raw, confident sexuality. And for the first time, I felt it. Felt those stirrings. Having never dealt with her kind before, I foolishly thought both those feelings and her interest were genuine.

"My world had been cold and dark for as long as I had existed. Night was a time of fear, isolation, and stifling quiet. But she showed me it could be a time for passion, for heat, for closeness. That quickly, my world expanded infinitely. She showed me new pleasures, and I must admit, I grew fond of her. Doted upon her. Allowed myself to be vulnerable in ways I otherwise never would have. I gave her my trust, my attention, my time...and in so doing, gave her power over me without realizing it. I was her prey. As an immortal, I was a bottomless well of sustenance for her.

"But I did not understand that at the time. Didn't recognize the signs that surely had been there all along. I knew only that I'd been somehow...kindled. Ignited from within. Made brighter. And at the peak of that feeling, she..." Nyte's shoulders rose as he drew in a deep breath, and his lips twitched to reveal his fangs when he exhaled harshly. "She tore out my heart, just as she'd planned all along."

Ember gasped softly, her eyes flaring. Surely he didn't mean... "She...tore out your heart?"

He held out a hand, palm toward the ceiling, and curled his fingers as though clutching something within them. "Right from my chest. And devoured it before my very eyes."

"Why?"

Nyte clenched his fist, and it trembled in the air. "Because her gluttony compelled her to. She'd fed from me for years by that point, and the more my heart brimmed with lust and affection, the more tempting it became to her. Why have a taste when she could gorge herself on an entire feast? Infused with my magic, with my stolen lifeforce, she became stronger than ever, and I doubt she would've had to feed again for a long, long while."

Ember gaped at him. "That fucking bitch!"

He looked at her, a crease forming between his eyebrows as he lowered his hand.

She clutched at her arms as anger burned in her chest for what had been done to him, for what he'd been through. He'd been so... God, he'd basically experienced a form of love for the first time, and the person he'd come to care for, the person he'd trusted, had literally stolen his heart from his chest and fucking *ate* it.

Ember attempted to temper the rage brimming within her. The succubus wasn't here, and there was nothing that could be done about her now.

"Is that why you secluded yourself in the Pit of Despair?" she asked gently. "It was because of her, wasn't it?"

"Yes. I was left...diminished. Vulnerable. I needed time to recover, time for my heart to regenerate."

Sadness washed through her, and she touched her fingers to her chest, unable to imagine what he must have felt. How alone he must have been.

Ember stepped toward him, wanting to touch him, needing to comfort him. "I am not Sarne—"

He cut her off with a hiss, eyes blazing. "No. Do not sully your lips with her accursed name."

"I'm not her, Nyte. I would never hurt you."

"I was foolish enough to give in to lust once before." Nyte straightened, both his body and expression hardening. "I will not do so again. I will not leave myself exposed to such a betrayal. I've no need for attachments, for caring and affection."

"You may say you don't need them, but I believe you want them. And more than that, I know you *deserve* to have them."

Crossing his arms, Nyte scowled and notched his chin up, spreading his wings behind him. "I am a nocturnus. I am darkness and emptiness given form."

Ember snorted at his air of superiority and gestured to her thighs, where his dried cum still sparkled. "You sure weren't empty when you came last night."

Nyte opened his mouth as though to speak, but his gaze dipped to her thighs, and no sound emerged. The light in his eyes brightened with the same heat, lust, and primal possessiveness that had been in them last night before he snapped them back up to meet hers. "I will not be mocked."

"I'm not mocking you, Nyte, I'm telling you the truth. We shared something last night. I felt it, and I know you felt it too. Your ex was evil, manipulative, and cruel, but you've already given her four hundred years. You shouldn't waste any more time because of her."

He clawed at his own chest. "What difference can time make to such a wound, mortal?"

Back to mortal, *huh?*

So much for him saying her name.

It's him trying to put distance between us.

"You're seriously going to give up on love because of some nasty succubus who wasn't worthy of your heart?" Ember asked.

"Love?" he scoffed, eyes flicking aside. "There's no such thing."

"There is, and I'll prove it." She closed the distance between them, and this time, he didn't disappear on her, didn't move away, though he remained wary.

She stroked her fingers down his cheek and along his jaw in

a gentle caress. As though unable to help himself, he subtly leaned into her touch, lashes drooping.

Smiling, Ember stood on her toes to brush her lips over his. "I'm not giving up on you, Nyte."

She withdrew and walked past him toward the bathroom, leaving him speechless as her lips tingled with the want for more.

Chapter Seventeen

Nyte lay back, propping himself on his elbows. The shingles were abrasive beneath him, but the discomfort provided no distraction from the guilt that had skewered his chest.

He sensed Ember's presence in the house below him. Fittingly, it was like a fire, radiating alluring heat. For so long, he'd felt like he was adrift in an icy abyss, bereft of warmth and light. All he had to do was go to her now and that ice would melt.

But instead, he was lying on her roof, staring up at a night sky in which the moon and stars were obscured by dark clouds and the city's artificial glow. Hiding in the one place within the tether's range to which she could not follow him.

An ageless nocturnus, hiding from a mortal.

That's what this was, no matter how adamantly he insisted otherwise. Not avoidance, not claiming personal space. Just simple cowardice. Because being near Ember made it too difficult for Nyte to do what was necessary. Too difficult to break this damnable attachment.

He lay down flat, closed his eyes, and laced his fingers

together, resting his hands on his belly. For what must've been the thousandth time, he recalled their exchange from a week ago.

I'm not giving up on you, Nyte.

And she hadn't. She'd remained kind, considerate, and affectionate, had continued speaking to him, smiling at him, and flirting with him at every opportunity. And he'd given her nothing in return.

This new distance between them mirrored the physical distance he'd sought tonight. A chasm had opened between them, a wide, yawning maw so deep and dark that it may as well have been bottomless. Every day, every moment, Ember strove to bridge that gap.

Her efforts had been fruitless because of Nyte. That chasm existed because of him, and he could not let it be crossed.

All the guilt and loneliness bristling inside him were his own fucking fault.

For seven days, he and Ember hadn't touched one another. Not even the lightest brush of fingertips. Nyte had made sure of it. He'd maintained space between them, had kept on the opposite side of the shop from her while she worked, and had pushed the tether's limits in her home, staying in different rooms. He hadn't eaten dinner or watched movies with her, and he'd walked behind her whenever they went out.

And he missed everything he was avoiding. Missed all those moments of connection and togetherness. Missed...her.

His skin thrummed with the desire to feel her, and that sensation only intensified with each inch of space between them. He was starved for her touch, craved the feel of her hands on him, of her lips against his own. Craved to be inside his witch.

Whenever he heard the shower turn on behind the closed bathroom door, he had to fight an overbearing ache low in his belly and turn all his willpower toward not joining Ember, toward not envisioning her naked body with water coursing over her smooth, pale skin. Even seeing her clothed was often too much. The way her garments hugged and accentuated her curves, the way her body moved, the way her hair framed her face, that luster in her eyes...it was all maddening.

Temptation stood in his path no matter which way he turned.

Baring his fangs, he lowered a hand to his groin, clamping it down to deter his cock from coalescing. How could his pelvis be throbbing when he had no veins, no blood, when he had a heart that did not beat?

Nights had proven the most difficult periods to weather. Seeing her lying in bed, serene and vulnerable, awoke an instinct in him to lie beside her, wrap her in his arms, wings, and tail, and shelter her through the darkness. And that instinct became overwhelming as the long, quiet nights wore on.

Despite what had occurred between Nyte and Ember and this prolonged aftermath, he'd had no choice but to accompany her while she worked and ran errands. He'd lapsed back into the security of keeping himself invisible to other humans, but it was only a small source of comfort.

Since he'd been quieter and more standoffish, she'd found a way to fill the silence. They'd twice gone to the library. Seeing so many books in one place, not as part of a wealthy mortal's private collection but available freely to the public, had been astounding.

Ember had borrowed numerous books concerning magic, witchcraft, spirituality, and demons, and had spent hours combing through them and researching corresponding subjects on her computer.

That was what she was doing right now—sitting on her bed

with a stack of books beside her and the laptop on her thighs, reading.

While he brooded on the roof.

Opening his eyes, Nyte sat up, bent his legs, and rested his arms on his knees. His tail thumped on the shingles behind him in a slow but restless rhythm.

He'd been determined to find Ember's boundless curiosity irritating, but he'd succeeded only in finding it endearing. She was actively seeking knowledge about her world, his world, and herself. Watching her sift through so much rubbish to unearth the scraps of truth buried within had only strengthened his admiration for her.

She was intelligent and adaptable, keeping a firm grip on her sense of self despite learning that so much of what she'd known had either been incomplete or incorrect.

If only you could follow her example, you damned fool.

He clenched his fists. He couldn't help but think of Sarnessa. The succubus had been unshakably self-assured, keenly aware of every asset at her disposal and exactly how to apply those tools. A sultry, seductive exterior hiding a cold, calculating core; feigned interest and intimacy masking ravenous selfishness. Sarnessa was an incarnation of the extreme beauty and cruelty in an uncaring, unjust universe.

She'd temporarily curtailed her cruelty to achieve her aim—gorging herself on Nyte's lifeforce. The only kindness she had shown him had been self-serving...and he'd only thought of it as kindness because he hadn't known better.

Ember was nothing like that. She had wants, of course she did, but she'd never treated them as more important than Nyte's. Though the summoning hadn't been intentional, she could've taken advantage. Could've attempted some pact with him to her own benefit, as so many humans had with other supernatural entities.

But she hadn't. She'd instead welcomed him into her home, treated him with caring and respect, had talked and joked and laughed with him. Ember made him feel not just wanted, but... worthy.

You're seriously going to give up on love because of some nasty succubus who wasn't worthy of your heart?

Those words stung in a way Nyte never could have anticipated not because of the past, but because of the present. Because of Ember.

Because he wanted nothing more than to give her his heart, and that was exactly why he had to resist. That he'd become so enamored with Ember as to willingly disregard the painful lessons he'd learned wasn't romantic, it was alarming.

Besides, once she had his heart, what need would she have for him again?

He told himself that such a notion ran against everything he knew about her, but he could shake neither the thought nor the unsettling sensation in his gut that accompanied it.

Nyte speared his fingers into his hair beside his horns, dragging his claws over his scalp. If only that bit of pain, or the chill in the air, or *anything* were enough to clear his mind and alleviate the fiery, crushing pressure in his chest.

Ten days...he needed to endure just ten more days, and then he would be free. Free to escape this torturous temptation, free to...

To wallow in despair?

Bowing his head, he lowered his gaze to the roof.

Was that really what he intended to do once the spell broke? Slink back into a dark pit, tail tucked between his legs, and waste away as eons crawled by?

When he felt the familiar arcane pulse that signaled Starling's arrival, he didn't bother lifting his head. "What do you want?"

The sprite's glow cast Nyte's shadow long and dark across the shingles, the shadow shrinking as she came closer.

"Why are you still up here moping?" Starling demanded. "You are wasting time, you foolish demon!"

Nyte's brow furrowed. There was something layered into her voice, something more than her impatience and annoyance. Was it...a hint of concern?

Starling fluttered to his front, calling his eyes to her, and planted her hands on her hips. "Go to her. Before I force you to do so."

Nyte tilted his head, studying his little friend. There was an odd urgency in her voice, an uncharacteristic tension in her posture. She'd appeared to him several times over the last week, repeatedly scolding him about his lack of progress with Ember, but she'd never seemed so off the other times.

"What's wrong?" he asked.

She thrust her hands out in an exasperated gesture. "You! Why are you so determined to let her slip through your fingers?"

But he was watching her closely now, and he didn't miss the tightness in her brow or the erratic twitch in the beating of her wings.

"Starling..."

The sprite offered an exaggerated shrug, turning her face away from him.

He lifted a hand and gently nudged her middle with a crooked finger. She grabbed the digit with two clawed hands, tensing as though to push it away, but stopped when he gently said, "Starling, please."

She squeezed his finger, let out a miniscule huff, and withdrew to hover back and forth in the air before him. "Fine. I did not want to speak of it, because you are moody enough already, but if you will not give me peace..."

Nyte's brows fell. There was so much there to which he could've responded, but he chose to let her continue. It was the easiest thing to do, and his existence had been sorely lacking ease for what felt like millennia.

"All right, so, you are no longer in the Pit of Despair, which is good, yes? Great even!" The sprite continued flitting back and forth, gesturing with all four hands as she spoke, only occasionally looking at him. "And you are even making progress. Finally breaking this shell you formed around yourself. Even if you are being *stubborn*."

She shot him a glare to emphasize that last word. "But you were there for a long, long time—in Despair, I mean—and your sudden absence has drawn some attention. And it is not that attention is a bad thing, because some attention is good, like the attention Ember shows you, but..."

Everything within Nyte stilled, and all sound faded from his perception. The tightness in his chest intensified to an impossible degree, and that old, bitter pain roared through him, clawing at his soul from within.

"But what?" he rasped, the words like broken glass slicing his throat.

Starling paused, arms falling to her sides, and drew in a deep breath. Her mouth opened as though she meant to speak again, but it was several seconds before anything came out, and her voice was particularly small when she spoke. "Sarnessa knows."

Nyte's hands curled into fists, claws biting into his palms. "Knows what?"

"That you are out. And she miiiight be looking for you..."

The surge of emotions that flooded Nyte was so powerful that he couldn't register what any of them were, leaving him stiflingly, torturously numb. "She either is or isn't."

The sprite winced, lips drawing back to reveal her tiny, pointed teeth, and hummed hesitantly. "Is."

Nyte growled. "Sun scorch me to fucking cinder."

"But"—Starling displayed all four palms placatingly—"she has not an inkling of where you are. So you need not worry, not at all. And if that succubitch shows up, I will make her regret that she ever touched you."

If Sarnessa was looking for him, it was only a matter of time before she found him. Only a matter of time before she came back and... What would she do? What could she possibly hope to accomplish? This time, he wouldn't be vulnerable and naïve. This time, he'd be on his guard, and he'd be ready to tear her asunder.

But Ember... His dear little witch had no defenses against any demon, much less an ancient succubus.

By all the hells, there was far too much left to chance here. Far too much left unknown. And the thought of Ember coming to any harm was like a spear of cold iron rammed up through his ribs and into his heart. That cold was offset by a firestorm of rage at his core, a roaring blaze threatening to break free. If Sarnessa touched Ember, if she so much as looked at Nyte's witch, he would inflict a thousandfold the suffering that he'd endured.

Though he felt like he was about to explode with all the pressure built up inside him, he forced himself to speak. "Help me keep vigil over this house. So long as I am bound to her, Ember is in danger. Sarnessa is not one to pass up a meal."

"What do you think I have been doing all this time?" the sprite replied with a toothy grin.

Nyte shook his head at her, unable to keep the corner of his mouth from twitching up. "Of course you've been playing voyeur all this while. What else should I have expected?"

Starling giggled. "I did say this would be entertaining."

"When this is through, I need to find new friends."

"You will not need new friends, Nyte. You will have your soulmate."

He could not bring himself to reply. That word felt too heavy, too potent, too...

Too right.

For the first time, Nyte understood what he was feeling. Understood firsthand the thing he'd inspired in mortals for so long.

Fear.

Chapter Eighteen

Ember turned off the television and tossed the remote aside. She could only rewind the movie so many times before accepting that she simply wasn't paying attention to it. The bed frame creaked quietly beneath her as she reached for one of the books on the nightstand, intending to read more about witches instead, but she withdrew her hand with a groan and flopped back onto the bed.

Her research didn't feel like it was going anywhere. She'd read about witches and their history, though most of the available records involved innocent people who'd been accused of practicing witchcraft rather than actual witches. She'd read about demons, incubi and succubae, and other entities from many cultures, but how was she to know what bits of the myths were based in fact?

As for Nyte's kind, the nocturni, there was nothing to be found. She suspected that they'd been lumped in with other creatures of the night in most of the old stories, twisted into fairy tales of boogey men and horrors haunting people's dreams.

She'd delved into books and sources online about witches and covens. There were covens all over the world—especially in Salem, which wasn't surprising. But again, how could she know where she belonged?

Some people embraced the witch aesthetic, enjoying crystals and incense and all things occult. Others considered themselves witches in a spiritual sense, focusing on intuition, inner wisdom, and devoting themselves to nature, whether practicing Paganism or more personal sets of beliefs.

Some covens seemed more like social groups, ways to bring women together in sisterhood. Others focused on building community around shared spirituality and rituals. Many covens partook in volunteer work and activism, seeking to improve their neighborhoods through their actions. And after sending out some inquiries, Ember learned that a few covens were quite secretive and selective in their membership, following strict rules and revealing very little to outsiders.

Which of those groups actually knew that demons like Nyte were real? Which of them knew how to cast spells, which could teach Ember to use the magic that was apparently in her blood? She doubted her parents knew anything about it, and she wasn't about to ring them up and ask.

Hey Mom, Dad, do you know if there are any witches in the family? Maybe Grandma had an old spellbook to pass down to me?

Ember was completely lost.

And she knew that if she tried to read tonight, it would be the same as watching the movie. Her eyes would skim over the words, but not a single one would register.

Her mind simply kept drifting to Nyte.

He was the only person she knew who could answer any of her questions. Except he was never around to do so.

Ember hated this distance between them. Hated that she

couldn't talk to him, couldn't enjoy a movie without him, couldn't even read without his presence.

She missed him.

Today had been even more brutal because she hadn't even had work to keep her occupied. She'd woken up alone and had spent her day all by herself in this big old house, neither seeing nor hearing from him at all.

Enough of this.

It'd been eight days of this nonsense. She wasn't going to let it continue.

Sitting up, Ember climbed out of bed and drew off her nightgown as she made her way to her dresser. Pulling out a pair of black leggings and an oversized black off-shoulder sweater, she dressed and put on socks before heading downstairs.

If Nyte wouldn't willingly come to her, she'd take matters into her own hands. Hell, she'd even forgone a bra hoping that he'd notice.

She grabbed her keys from the kitchen and tucked them in her pocket as she made her way to the front door. Shoving her feet into her black combat boots, she zipped up the sides, stood, and stepped outside, striding along the walkway toward the sidewalk.

Ember smiled, silently counting each step away from her property.

"Where in the hells are you going at this hour of the night?" Nyte demanded from directly behind her.

She couldn't stop her lips from stretching into a grin as she came to a halt.

Worked like a charm.

"Oh, just going on a midnight stroll," she said cheerily, turning to face him.

His expression was furious, with his brows angled sharply

down over those smoldering eyes, his lips pressed in a tight line, and his nostrils flared. "It's not safe to be out here alone."

"But I'm not alone, am I? It's so thoughtful of you to join me." She moved to Nyte's side, wrapped her arms around one of his, making sure to press her breasts against him, and peered up at him with a sweet smile. "I know you'll protect me from all the things that go bump in the night. Well, all the *other* things."

A shudder rippled through his tense body, and his wings quivered as he released a heavy breath. But he didn't *poof* away. That was more than she'd hoped for with the way he'd been acting lately. She could feel his tail swinging behind them as though in irritation.

With an exaggerated, exasperated flick of his wrist, he waved her forward.

Before her foot had even come down with her first step, clothing appeared on his body. Though his demonic features remained, she knew he wouldn't appear that way for anyone else who looked at him.

And she wouldn't appear to have lost her mind walking with her arms looped around thin air.

"See, isn't this nice?" she asked. "A quiet night, fresh air—well, fresh-ish air—and pleasant company."

Nyte grunted in a way that sounded rather skeptical.

Ember narrowed her eyes. "You *do* like my company, right? Because I would hate to think you used me for sex just to ghost me afterward. I might have to hex your shadowy ass."

He sighed and shook his head. "Firstly, I'm a nocturnus, not a ghost. Secondly, you don't know how to cast any hexes. And thirdly, we both know which of us is pleasant company and which is not."

She chuckled. "I'm sure I could learn how to cast a hex or two." Reaching up, she brushed a lock of curls from his brow. "Also, I do adore your grumpy demeanor. It's cute."

"Cute?" His head snapped toward her, the agitation in his expression replaced by incredulity. "I'm a demon formed of darkness, witch. I'm not *cute*. I am everything you mortals fear in the dead of night."

Ember pinched his cheek, and in a saccharine voice said, "Aww, look at you trying to be all mean and scary."

His features fell into a droll look. "I cannot help but feel my existence is plummeting toward a new low."

"Oh, don't be so glum." She slipped her arm back around his, hugging it as they continued walking. "Enjoy the night with me. You've been way too distant lately."

"And this is your answer to that?"

"It's working, isn't it?"

He grunted again. "It shouldn't be."

"But it did because you're worried about me. Because you care about me. Don't you?"

And considering that he was letting her touch him, letting her hold on to him, maybe he'd been just as starved for contact as Ember.

"Despite myself," he said through clenched teeth, "I do."

Warmth bloomed in her chest. She hadn't realized just how much her heart had ached in his absence, how cold and hollow it had felt, until now.

Ember smiled and rested her head against his arm. They were moving away from the city center, away from the people, the noise, the lights. As they walked, Nyte's tail occasionally brushed her legs, and once it even started curling around her waist before he abruptly withdrew it.

Gradually, the tension bled from Nyte, and he relaxed.

She gazed up at the sky through the boughs of the trees lining the sidewalk. Though it was mostly clear, with the moonlight illuminating a few lazily drifting clouds, there were barely any stars to be seen.

"The sky here isn't the same as in Nebraska," she said softly. "You can't see the stars as clearly. I think that's what I miss the most since moving here. Being able to look up and see the whole universe there, with more stars than you can count."

Nyte tipped his head back to gaze upward. He was silent for a time before he spoke. "I know you're not afraid of the dark, witch. What about heights?"

Ember looked at him, at the sharp angle of his jaw, at his straight, narrow nose and the sinful curve of his lips. Moonlight fell upon his skin, making the motes upon it sparkle, and glinted off his earrings. Once more, she was struck by how beautiful he was. "I'm not afraid of heights."

"Good." In a flash, he swept Ember off her feet into a bridal carry, drawing her against his chest. She had scarcely enough time to let out a startled gasp and wrap her arms around his neck before his wings flared out and he leapt off the ground.

"Oh my God, Nyte!" Her stomach sank as they gained altitude, and she tightened her grip on him.

His clothes dissipated like smoke. Wind rushed around her, fluttering her hair and sweater, sweeping beneath her clothing to chill her skin. And she watched as the ground and the city grew farther and farther away.

Before long, Salem sprawled out below them, the straight lines of its well-lit streets juxtaposed by the dark waters of Salem Harbor butting against them.

"I've not brought you up here for you to stare at the world below," Nyte said, his voice cutting through the whooshing air.

Ember dragged her shocked gaze up to Nyte, blinking against the wind. He was regarding her with a playful smirk. Oh, how she'd missed those smiles of his.

When he came to a stop, with the shadows of his wings billowing behind him, she looked beyond Nyte to the dark, starlit sky. Her eyes widened and her lips parted in wonder.

From up here, it looked nothing like it had on the street below.

The heavens were midnight blue spattered with subtle nebulas in violet and pink, all backing countless glittering stars. The waxing moon hung lower in the sky, pure silver and larger than she'd ever seen it.

"You brought me to see the stars," Ember whispered.

"And you shine brighter than all of them, Ember."

Breath catching and heart quickening, she met his gaze. His eyes glowed ethereally, hints of the same blues and purples that were in the surrounding sky swirling around cores of pure white starlight. The warmth in her chest expanded, spreading through her body and coaxing her closer to him. He'd rarely said her name, and each time he'd done so had been profound. That he was saying it now, after days of keeping his distance, nearly brought tears to her eyes.

Her attention flicked to his mouth. "Nyte..."

His fingers flexed, the bite of his claws only reminding her of the pleasure they'd shared and making her ache to experience it again. There was a possessiveness in his hold that was reinforced when his tail swung up to coil around her calf. Shadows coalesced around her, cocooning her in their whispery embrace, their insubstantial wisps somehow blocking out the chill.

Nyte's eyes lingered on hers, blazing with heat, beckoning her closer, closer...

Please... Please, kiss me.

He abruptly looked away. His wings pumped, launching them forward through the sky. A thrill raced through Ember, tickling her belly, and she squeaked, holding on tight. But she had no need to worry. Nyte held her close, his arms banded around her in a firm, unwavering grip. He wouldn't let her fall.

Her hair whipped around her head, and though the air was

cold on her face and arms, the shadows surrounding her kept her warm.

They soared through the sky, flying amidst a sea of stars and moonlight. It was magical. And it was a gift he'd given to her because he'd heard the longing in her voice. Nyte might have tried to distance himself from her, to stop whatever bond was forming between them, but this was a sign that he was failing in that endeavor.

He didn't have to do any of this for her. Didn't have to let her take his arm as they walked, didn't have to respond to anything she said, and he certainly didn't have to take her flying and share this dazzling, breathtaking view. But he'd done it all anyway, and he'd done it for her.

Smiling, Ember let go of Nyte's neck to reach out as though she could touch the stars overhead despite knowing how far away they still were.

"Such things are not for mortal hands to hold," Nyte rumbled.

She chuckled as she pretended to curl her fingers around one of the stars and bring it to his chest, flattening her palm there. "Then you can hold it for me."

His eyes met hers, and something softened in them. Her belly fluttered, and it had nothing at all to do with the fact that they were flying.

"Take care with your wishes, mortal...lest they come true."

Chapter Nineteen

Shadows enveloped Ember, blotting out the sky and reducing her world only to Nyte. His embrace didn't falter even through the fleeting nothingness that followed. He remained real and solid, her anchor, her rock.

Then the shadows whisked away to reveal her bedroom, which Nyte was now standing in, still cradling her in his arms. The sudden change of location should've been disorienting, but he kept her grounded. Somehow, he'd done so even while they'd been soaring across the night sky.

When he lowered her onto her feet and attempted to pull away, Ember tightened her hold around his neck and pressed her forehead to his.

"Don't go. Please," she begged. "Stay with me."

His hands fell to her hips, fingers curling as though he was unable to relinquish his hold. "I can't."

"You're only telling yourself that because you're afraid." Drawing her head back, she met his gaze and touched her palm to his chest. "But I'll never take anything from you that you don't offer freely, Nyte."

Clenching his jaw, he flicked his eyes to her hand. Though he said nothing, she knew he was warring with himself. The battle was clear in his expression, in the tension radiating through his body, and in the agitated flicking of his tail.

Ember released him and stepped away, not taking her eyes off him as she toed off her boots and pushed her pants down her legs, kicking them aside. Slowly moving backward toward the bed, she grasped the hem of her sweater and pulled it off over her head, tossing it to the floor as her hair fell back into place around her shoulders.

Nyte's blazing, cosmic gaze dropped to her body, and there was no mistaking the hunger in it. His stare was so intense that Ember felt it on her skin, felt its searing path as it trailed over her breasts, lingering on her nipples, and dipped down her belly to her pussy. He drew in a shuddering breath, lips parting to reveal the tips of his fangs.

The stark, predatorial glint in his eyes sent a rush of pure, unadulterated lust through her, heating her core. She wanted his hands on her, his mouth, his teeth. Wanted his kisses, wanted to feel his cock thrusting inside her body. Wanted him to claim her, to possess her utterly.

Wanted him to...love her.

If Nyte were to leave her now, Ember would've been crushed. She knew she was running out of time to prove what she felt. To prove that he felt it toward her, too.

Sitting on the edge of her bed, she leaned back, propped herself up on one arm, and slowly parted her legs, feeling the air brush against her hot sex. Her eyes didn't leave her demon as she slid her fingers up the inside of her right thigh, running them over the scar left behind by his fangs. And his gaze followed their movements.

A low growl rumbled in his chest.

"Don't you want me, Nyte?" Ember asked.

"Ember..." There was warning in his tone, but there was also a primal, tantalizing ravenousness.

"This can be yours," she said softly, gliding her fingers through her pussy and lightly stroking her labia. She was already wet for him, with her slick coating her folds and nearly dripping down to her ass. "I can be yours."

Nyte's tail thrashed behind him. His gaze remained focused upon her pussy, ardently watching, and the stars on his body were growing brighter. He drew in a deep breath, nostrils flaring like those of a predator scenting its prey.

Ember circled her clit. A breathy sigh escaped her as whispers of pleasure flitted through her body. She let her head tip back, let her back arch, but she didn't look away from Nyte. Seeing him in this state was erotic as hell. The tension in his body as he struggled to withstand temptation, the flaming desire in his eyes, the desperate, consuming want. A lustful beast had roused within him, and it was exciting beyond words.

The sensation within Ember sharpened with every brush against her clit. She longed for it to be his fingers touching her rather than her own.

"You can have all of me, Nyte." She parted her thighs wider, her breaths coming short and shallow. "You can have me any way you want me."

Ember slid her hand down and thrust her middle finger deep inside her pussy, pumping it in and out, hearing exactly how wet she was. "You can fuck me."

Nyte bared his fangs and took a step forward only to jerk to a halt again, the cords of his neck straining. Darkness gathered at his groin, and she watched, transfixed, as it formed into his cock, with its sculpted head and the angled ridges running along its shaft. Her pussy clenched at the memory of how they'd felt inside her.

Withdrawing her finger, she skimmed it up her body,

leaving a trail of her slick as it ran along her belly, over her breast, and circled her nipple. "You can taste me."

Ember closed her lips around her finger and sucked away her arousal.

"You wicked witch," he bit out. A drop of glittering silver cum seeped from the tip of his cock.

Slowly, she pulled her finger free, tracing her bottom lip with it as her mouth curved into a smile. "You can keep me, Nyte. Forever."

Suddenly, Nyte was immediately in front of her. She had no idea whether he'd simply moved faster than her eyes could perceive or had teleported, only that he was right there, his hands taking her hips in an iron grip that pressed his claws into her flesh.

Shadows swirled around her, and the world disappeared for an instant, though his hold on her remained as solid and sure. When they reappeared, he was no longer in front of Ember, but beneath her, with her ass on his chest and her knees on either side of his head.

Ember's eyes flared as they met his burning, starlit gaze.

Curling his hands around her thighs, he dragged her forward until her pussy was over his face. "This cunt is fucking *mine*."

And then his mouth was on her.

Ember gasped as he latched on to her clit, giving it a rough, sharp suck that sent a burst of pleasure through her. Her hands floundered, unsure of what to grasp, until they finally dropped to his horns. She gripped them tight, brow furrowing as the overwhelming sensation built and built, making her toes curl.

"Oh, oh fuck! Nyte!" she cried, eyes squeezing shut.

Right before she would've come, he released her clit, and his hot, delectable tongue swept between her folds. A shudder coursed through her, and her clit pulsed in the aftermath, aching from the orgasm he'd denied her.

"No!" she gasped. "No, no, no."

He growled, the vibrations rolling into her an instant before he plunged his long tongue inside her pussy. Her inner walls clenched around the sweet invasion. His claws dug into her skin as he impaled her with his tongue, as it darted in and out in quick, deep thrusts, twisting and curling, hitting every sensitive spot within her.

Then his mouth was back on her clit, his tongue and lips lavishing it with slow, lingering nips and circular strokes. She could feel the scrape of his fangs against her tender flesh, and that only added to the thrill of it, making her belly flutter.

And all she could do was writhe above him, as his hands were banded firmly over her legs, keeping her in place while he devoured her pussy with those otherworldly eyes never wavering.

Soft wisps brushed along her skin as shadows drifted off him to touch seemingly every part of her.

Ember panted, rasping his name over and over, unable to keep still. She needed more pressure, more friction, more of him. Everything about this moment, everything about Nyte was overwhelming, but it was never enough. It never would be. She would always want more.

Heat spread through her body, her skin tingled, her pelvis rocked, and her thighs trembled. She tightened her grip on his horns. She was so, so close.

When the sensations became too staggering, she fell forward onto her hands and rode his face, inhibitions vanishing. All that existed was Nyte and the pleasure roiling within her. Her breasts swayed beneath her, and her moans filled the room as she grinded against him.

The sounds he made were bestial, snarls, growls, and grunts

from deep in his chest that vibrated against her pussy, enhancing the feel. His tongue lashed her clit quickly, brutally, again and again and again.

Clutching her thighs, Nyte pulled her down firmly, closed his lips over her clit, and sucked.

Ember's body went taut as stars careened into her, stealing her breath, her thoughts, her vision. A keen burst from her throat, escalating into high-pitched cries. Her body spasmed as wave after wave of ecstasy assailed her, and though she tried to escape the onslaught, Nyte kept her trapped against his mouth.

"Nyte!" she begged, tears stinging her eyes from the intensity of it, but he did not relent. Not until she was taken by another orgasm that forced a rush of liquid heat from her.

Chapter Twenty

Nyte drank from Ember as she came. He held her legs in place, not allowing her cunt out of reach as he lapped up every drop of her essence and coaxed yet more from her. She trembled atop him, her thighs quaking on either side of his head, and her impassioned, desperate cries filled the air in the most arousing song he'd ever heard.

He should've been satisfied with that nectar. Should've been sated. How many could say they had sampled something so pure, so heavenly? To seek more from her would've been selfish, greedy, gluttonous.

But his raging need was far too powerful for him to care about such things. The potential pain and suffering, that vulnerability, none of it mattered. Ember was everything now, and he would not deny himself further.

Snarling, he tore his mouth from her. Her slick dripped down his chin, and his tongue darted out to lick it away. Her scent flooded his nose, leaving room for no others, and he breathed it in hungrily.

In a torrent of shadows, he vanished from beneath Ember and rematerialized behind her. On her hands and knees, she turned her head immediately to look at him over her shoulder, her eyes half-lidded and glossy with pleasure and desire.

She looked at him with as much need as he felt. A mortal, matching his appetite. By all the hells, she was perfect.

His dear little witch.

Nyte caught her hips between his hands, angled his pelvis to press the head of his cock against her dripping cunt, and slammed into her. She gasped, arms shaking, even as he growled. Her tender flesh yielded beneath his claws as her inner walls squeezed.

Pleasure spiraled up from his groin to race out through the rest of his body. Nothing felt as good as Ember. Nothing had ever—would ever—come close. That was the one unmalleable truth of the universe.

Keeping firm hold of her, he drove into her again and again, hard and fast, pushing his cock ever deeper and his pleasure ever higher. His tail coiled around her thigh, its tip pressing into her folds and stroking her clit in time with his pumping hips. Shadows spread from his body, extensions of his being, of his soul, to brush her skin and tease her nipples.

And still he sped his pace, still he thrust with increasing strength, making the pressure low in his belly build and build. With his hands, his shaft, his tail and shadows, he felt all of Ember, felt her every reaction, every tremor that coursed through her, every breath she sucked in, every thump of her racing heart, and he needed more still. Forever more.

It wasn't enough to feel her. Nyte needed to be one with her. To imprint himself upon her, body and soul, so they could never be disentangled. So they would never be apart again.

Take her.

He hammered into her, making her cry out.

Claim her.

His claws bit into her skin as he drew her back onto his cock, thighs slapping.

Keep her.

Nyte's tail firmly pressed down on her clit and vibrated.

Mine.

With a broken scream, Ember fell forward, arms giving out beneath her. Her ass lifted higher, the angle increasing the friction between their moving bodies, and new pleasure pulsed along his shaft.

She clutched the blanket, turning her face to rest it on her cheek as her breath blew wild strands of silver hair away. Her eyes were closed, her lips parted, her cheeks flushed. She was more beautiful with each moment.

And Nyte did not relent. He pistoned his hips, and her body drew him in, tight and hungry and slick.

His eyes dipped. He watched his dark cock, sparkling with tiny stars and coated in her essence, move in and out of her pink flesh, which stretched to accommodate him and clenched to keep him buried within. A growl tore from his chest at the sight.

Mine.

His gaze lifted to the rosette above her pussy. He needed to fill her completely, to make her know she was his, that he possessed all of her. His shadows stretched from his groin and pushed inside her ass, forming his second cock. He groaned at the tightness of her flesh around his. As he pumped his hips, he could feel the ridges of one cock against the underside of the other, both filling her so thoroughly, separated only by her flesh.

"Oh God," she moaned, clawing at the bedding even as she shoved her backside toward Nyte to take in more of him.

Nyte thrust into her again and again, his breaths raw and heavy as pleasure spiraled through him and coiled around his heart, his mind, his soul, squeezing as tightly as her body was squeezing his shafts. His thighs clapped against hers, the sound mingling with her escalating cries.

"You are mine, Ember," he grated. "You belong to *me*."

With his shadows curling and pinching her nipples and his tail thrumming against her clit, he lifted a hand from her hip and smacked her ass. The crack of skin against skin rose over the other sounds, sharp and piercing and wholly satisfying.

"Nyte!" she gasped.

Gods, he loved the sound of his name from her lips.

He savored her frantic moans, savored the way her ass and cunt gripped his cocks so sweetly and greedily, savored the way her soft body jiggled with his every brutal thrust, the way she tried to meet him despite the sensations clearly overwhelming her.

Her movements faltered, and her cunt clamped down on him, gushing hot cum as she cried out a wordless benediction.

A roar tore from Nyte's chest as the dam within him finally broke. His essence erupted from his cocks, and rapture exploded through him, threatening to unmake his form. Wings snapping out wide, he buried himself as deep inside her as he could with one final thrust, his fingers flexing on her hips.

Somehow, he kept his eyes open. All he could see was Ember; just her against a backdrop of stars dancing through the darkness, billions of pinpoints of light in the void, all flaring until his vision was swallowed by pure, blinding white.

Nyte banded an arm around Ember's middle and pulled her torso up, drawing her back against his chest. His other arm snaked around her, and he caught her throat, his fingers tipping her head back and turning her face toward him.

Their eyes met. There was no denying that the fires in hers were far more than lust, no denying the emotion with which she was looking at him. It radiated into him, pouring from her very being.

And the same emotion pulsed in his chest in response, a perfect reflection.

"Forever," he rasped before pressing his lips to hers in a possessive, claiming kiss.

Chapter Twenty-One

Ember stood bent over the counter with her arms folded atop it, smiling as she watched Nyte speak to a customer across the shop who was gesturing at Nyte's clothing. To the man, Nyte appeared human, and he was currently modelling one of the outfits that normally adorned a mannequin. But to Ember, he was the gorgeous, starlit demon he'd always been.

And fuck was he sexy.

A black and purple corset vest accentuated his narrow waist, showing off his broad chest and wide shoulders, and the black shirt beneath it perfectly molded to his lean, muscled arms. Ember's gaze ran down his body, and she caught her bottom lip between her teeth. Those black trousers hugged his thighs and taut ass.

Even knowing what lay beneath them, his clothes made her yearn to peel them off and reveal his sinfully hot body an inch at a time. She shifted, rubbing her thighs together as desire kindled in her core.

The past several days had been a complete one-eighty from the prior week. Nyte had rarely left her side, had barely been able to keep his hands off her. The night he'd taken her flying, when he'd finally given in to their mutual lust and longing, he'd stayed with her in bed until she'd fallen asleep. He'd stayed *inside* her. And it'd been that way every night since.

Ember's pussy and ass clenched with the memory of his cocks, the sensations still fresh from what they'd done this morning before coming to the boutique.

As though sensing her thoughts, Nyte glanced her way. His violet-blue eyes flashed with heat, and the corner of his mouth curved up into a smirk. There was a devilish promise in that brief look that sent a rush of want through her.

I can't wait until closing.

Someone cleared their throat near Ember.

Startled her from her ogling, she straightened and looked at the woman standing on the other side of the counter, who waited with an armful of items.

"I'm so sorry," Ember rushed to say, gesturing to the counter. "You can set all that here."

The woman chuckled as she laid down the skirt, handbag, and jewelry she'd been holding. Leaning forward, she pointed discreetly toward Nyte. "I don't blame you. He's hot."

Ember grinned.

And he's mine.

Though that wasn't true, was it? Maybe he was hers for now, but when the full moon rose in five days, he'd be released from the spell binding them together. He'd be free to leave her.

The happiness that had been burning bright inside Ember snuffed out. She forced her smile to remain in place as she chatted with the woman and rang up the items.

"Oh, and this." The woman plucked up the last pack of incense sticks from the basket next to the register. "I love these."

"They're my favorite too."

Especially since the spicy, woodsy scent reminded her of Nyte.

Once the woman paid and left the store, Ember looked back at Nyte. The man was still chatting with him, chuckling loudly at something Nyte had said. For as curmudgeonly as he often acted, the demon really could be charming when he wanted to be, and he'd taken to interacting with customers in the shop with an ease and enthusiasm that continued to surprise her.

Since there was no one else currently in the store, Ember took the opportunity to head into the back room and get some more incense to restock the basket. She rose on her toes, grabbed the box on one of the upper shelves, and pulled it down.

"Finally!" remarked a high-pitched voice.

Ember yelped, the box slipping from her grasp, as a tiny glowing figure flitted beside her. She fumbled, desperate to keep the box from falling to the floor. Once she'd clutched it tight against her chest, she looked at the sprite. "Starling?"

Starling grinned as she landed atop the box. "Who else would it be?"

A shiver ran through Ember. She hoped she'd never have to learn firsthand how razor-sharp those teeth really were. At a glance, one would think Starling was a fairy from a fairytale, delicate and beautiful, but there was a menacing edge to her beauty. Maybe it was the uncanniness of her more inhuman features, like her third eye, her elongated proportions, and her extra set of arms.

She was a bit unsettling up close.

"I'm just surprised," Ember said. "I haven't seen you since that first night."

Starling chuckled. "Oh, but I have seen plenty of you."

Ember arched a brow. "What does that mean?"

The sprite waved her upper right hand dismissively. "I have been waiting to speak with you alone, which has been difficult since the two of you have been inseparable these last few days. Not that I am complaining. I have waited centuries for Nyte to drag himself out of Despair and live again, and my is he *living*. You have certainly brought out something new in him, witchling. Seeing the two of you, hearing the two of you…"

She grinned wider and fanned herself.

Ember gaped at her. "Wait, wait, wait, wait. You've been watching us have sex?"

Starling rolled her eyes. "You mortals are so uptight. But no, I did not stay to watch. I simply check in from time to time. I am…keeping guard, you could say. Which is why I must speak to you."

"Why me and not Nyte?"

"Because this is something only you can do." Starling flitted up to hover in the air in front of Ember. "Did Nyte tell you Sarnessa is looking for him?"

Ember's stomach dropped. How long had Nyte known? And why…why hadn't he told her?

She looked down, clutching the box. Did he…still have feelings for the succubus? He'd spent four-hundred years in self-imposed exile to overcome the pain of her betrayal. He would've still been there had Starling not invoked the summoning through Ember. He'd said it was because he had been left vulnerable, because he'd needed time for his heart to recover. But that didn't mean he harbored no feelings for the succubus who'd awoken so much inside him.

"No," Ember said with a shake of her head as she slid the box onto a shelf. "Nyte didn't tell me."

Starling moved closer and placed a hand beneath Ember's chin, lifting it, forcing Ember to look at her. She was surprisingly strong despite her diminutive stature. "I know what thoughts are traipsing through your head, witchling. Cast them aside and set them ablaze so they never return. He carries only hatred for her. If he did not tell you, it is because he did not want to frighten you."

"Then why are you telling me?"

"To prepare you, because she will come. What she stole from him before she will try to take again. She covets its power, and it will be especially potent now. So I have a boon to bestow upon you. Something to use against that succubitch."

Starling flew to Ember's shoulder, placing her mouth near Ember's ear, and whispered words that Ember couldn't understand. Words that resonated with untold power, sending a chill down Ember's spine even as they sparked an electric tingling in her fingers and toes that crackled up her limbs.

And though it didn't make any sense, though it wasn't how reality was supposed to work, she felt those words take root in her mind. It felt like simply hearing them made them part of her, like she could call upon them whenever she needed.

When Starling finished, she drifted back with a smile. "Recite that incantation against her."

Ember touched her fingers to her chest, where she felt magic swirling inside her, ancient and mysterious. "You want me to cast a spell against a succubus?"

Starling nodded with a grin. "Send her straight to hell."

"I don't know if I can do this. I don't even know how I summoned Nyte to begin with. I was sleeping!"

"Ah, witchling. You have the power in you. You were never taught to harness it, but it is there, and it is yours to command. And when the moment comes... I believe you will know what to do with it."

Ember's brow furrowed. All of this was so new to her. Things she'd thought were make-believe, things that should've existed only in fantastical fiction, had become part of her reality. Why would she ever have thought that she could cast spells? That she was a witch?

I'm seriously going to need to have a talk with my family.

The curtain into the storeroom was swept aside, revealing Nyte in the doorway. His eyes flicked to Starling. "I thought I felt your presence here, sprite. What mischief are you making now?"

"Mischief?" Starling scoffed. She pressed the side of her face to Ember's cheek, her wings fluttering against Ember's hair. "I am simply having a chat with our lovely witchling."

One of his dark brows arched. "*Our?*"

She pouted and flitted over to Nyte, crossing her arms. "You are such a possessive nocturnus."

He smiled at her, his bared fangs conveying little warmth. "With all the watching you do, you've surely heard my claims on this mortal. She is mine."

A light, tinkling giggle escaped the sprite. "And I am overjoyed to hear it." She patted his cheek with both of her tiny left hands. "I must take my leave. So much to do, you understand. Ta-ta!"

The sprite disappeared, leaving behind a little cloud of fading stardust.

Quirking a brow, Ember crossed her arms, cocked her hip, and looked at Nyte. "How long have you known Starling was watching us?"

Chuckling, he walked toward Ember, wrapped his arms around her, and drew her against his chest. "From the beginning, but it doesn't matter. She was always going to watch her little scheme unfold whether we knew it or not."

He curled a finger around a lock of her hair as he lowered his face, skimming the tip of his nose over hers, his lips teasingly close to her own. "Regardless, she's not watching us right now..."

His hands smoothed down to her ass, trailing heat, and began bunching up her short skirt, exposing more of her thighs little by little.

Ember's breath hitched, and she grabbed his forearms to stop him. "Nyte! The store's open. Someone could walk in."

"I locked the door and turned the sign." Nyte dipped his head farther and grazed her neck with his fangs, making her shiver. "I need you. Now."

He opened his mouth wide and bit down.

The flare of pain forced a cry from her lips, but it was swiftly carried away on a rising tide of pleasure. Ember lifted her hands and slipped her fingers into his hair to clutch the dark locks. She held him closer as pleasure shot through her, going straight to her clit and making it pulse.

His fingers flexed, curling around her ass, pressing his claws into her flesh.

"Nyte," she moaned, each gentle pull from his mouth making her core clench as the hollow ache within her grew. A breathless laugh slipped past her lips. "You said you weren't a vampire."

He withdrew his fangs, and his tongue slid across the wounds, making them tingle and grow warmer. With a chuckle, he lifted his head to meet her gaze. "So long as it gets me another taste of you, I'll be whatever I must."

Nyte slanted his mouth over hers in a hungry kiss, pressing her back against the wall. She tasted blood on his tongue, mixed with the flavor of him, and God, why was that so titillating? He lifted her off her feet, parting her thighs wide, and she wrapped her legs around his hips as she returned the kiss, parting her lips and welcoming his sinful tongue.

His tail trailed along the back of her thigh, curling in to slide beneath her underwear. Ember whimpered as it brushed over her pussy. She felt the material being tugged to the side, felt air against her heated center, and then Nyte's cock was there, its head nudging against her.

With a growl, he pushed inside her, slowly, deeply, his girth stretching her, his length filling her, and Ember gasped against his mouth. As he'd said, he was made to fit her perfectly.

Nyte's eyes blazed with fierceness and possessiveness, holding her gaze captive as he thrust inside her, gradually bringing them both toward the heights of rapture. Neither of them looked away even when the universe began to shatter around them.

Chapter Twenty-Two

Though he heard the shower running in the bathroom, heard the sprays and splashes as Ember moved beneath the water, for once, Nyte's mind wasn't occupied by imaginings of her naked form. Not that he needed to imagine anymore after ten days of shared showers.

Instead, his attention was focused outside.

He lay atop Ember's bed, staring out the window at the rapidly darkening evening sky. There were no clouds today. The last daylight persisted stubbornly to the west, bleeding from muted orange to purple to black above the buildings blocking his line of sight.

The shower turned off. What silence it left was soon enough filled by the whine of Ember's hair dryer.

Nyte's tail thumped on the blanket in a lazy, heavy rhythm. Humans considered patience a virtue. He tended to agree; immortality must've been insufferable to anyone lacking it. But his was much thinner than usual tonight.

Waiting for Ember would always feel this way. He knew it with impossible certainty, and no part of him could dispute the fact. Whenever she was out of sight, he felt a gaping hole in his chest, a void so terribly cold and empty that it burned. He rubbed at it now despite knowing his touch could not soothe it.

And that feeling was exasperated by the other thing he was awaiting.

The moon.

The binding magic roiled within him, responding to the residual power of the full moon that would rise tonight, almost as though the enchantment were as eager to be dispelled as he was to be rid of it. Because once Nyte was free...

His fingers twitched, scraping his claws over his chest, and his tail slapped down hard.

Freedom... What did it mean to him now? For while he'd only been trapped with Ember for a month, his imprisonment had lasted much, much longer than that. What was freedom? What did it entail?

Choice. Ultimately, freedom was the power to choose.

Emotions swirled inside him, powerful, primal emotions that seemed to contradict one another. Light and dark, fire and ice, loud and deafeningly quiet. And Ember was at the core of all of them. She was at the core of Nyte.

He folded his hands together over his belly, pressing them down.

Lust. That was what he felt for Ember, wasn't it? Consuming, mind-clouding lust, and he'd allowed it to metamorphose into obsession. Acting upon those desires only inflamed them.

He'd experienced a deluge of lust with Sarnessa. He knew its feel, its flavor. He recognized it in himself now, albeit a hundredfold purer and stronger than anything the succubus had roused in him.

Because it's not mere lust, not simple obsession...

Nyte breathed deep. He could taste nightfall on the air, could feel the lunar magic of the coming moon thrumming all around him. But it paled in comparison to this thing inside him. This immense, complex emotion that had spread into every mote of his being.

This enthralling, all-encompassing thing, at once so overt and so subtle, this feeling that was unlike anything he'd ever felt, anything he could ever have conceived, that ran so vast and deep. Wonderful and terrible and frightening and inspiring.

No, it wasn't merely lust or obsession, not even close. This was new, and though he didn't know how to hold it, how to tend it, he knew what it was called.

This was two souls reaching for each other across an unfathomable, unforgiving abyss. Two hearts drawn together by a force stronger than any other bond, whether magical or physical, transcending even fate.

This...was love.

He recalled the word Starling had used.

Soulmate.

And tonight, when the magical tether binding him to Ember dissolved beneath the glow of the full moon, he had a choice to make. He had to define what freedom meant to him, what it would look like...

As he lay here contemplating it, he was increasingly sure of what he wanted it to be. Of what he wanted to give his dear little witch.

Tonight, he would gift her—

"My beautiful Nyte."

That familiar, seductive voice resonated around Nyte. It swept through him, invading his senses, his body, his mind. Once, it would've enticed him, would've aroused him. Would've had him on his knees eager to obey.

Now it only made his skin crawl and his shadows roil.

Sarnessa's scent enveloped him, fragrant and enticing. He felt weight pressing down on his pelvis and the brush of hair over his shoulders before she appeared over him, straddling his hips, her arms caging his head on either side.

Her pitch-black eyes stared into Nyte's as she smiled. "Hello, my love."

Sarnessa lowered her head, dropping her full, dark lips toward his.

Nyte shoved her off, dissipating to shadow in the same instant and rematerializing himself several feet away from the bed. His entire being buzzed with alarm, with wrongness, with fury.

She laughed, lying on her back atop the bed with her knees bent and thighs parted. All her crimson skin was on display. Curved black horns jutted from her long, raven hair, which was spread around her head.

She arched her back, clawed toes digging into the bedding as she ran her hands up her chest to cup her breasts and frame her hard, dark red nipples. "Ah, my Nyte, how I've missed you."

He clenched his fists at his sides, battling the impulse to clutch at his chest, which throbbed with echoes of that old pain. "The feeling isn't mutual, and I am *not* yours."

Sarnessa stuck her bottom lip out in a pout as she turned onto her side, propping her head on her palm. "You're still angry with me?"

"That's much too mild a word."

"You were in the Pit of Despair for four hundred years. Had I known, I would have gone to you sooner to rectify what happened. To explain." Her expression turned sultry. "To make it up to you."

"To explain?" He laughed humorlessly, tail slashing the air as shadows coalesced around him. "I should tear the still-beating heart from your chest and shove it down your throat. You can explain while you choke on it."

Her dark brows furrowed, and she pushed herself up, slipping off the bed to stand. "Do you know what it's like to be a slave to hunger? To feel that relentless, gnawing ache, to be tormented by an unquenchable thirst from the very first moment of your existence?"

Sarnessa approached him, her hips and breasts swaying sensually. "You sated that hunger, my love. Left me feeling so *full*. Didn't you want that for me? To end my suffering?"

"What of my suffering, Sarnessa?" Nyte demanded. The room darkened around him.

With a sigh, she flicked a hand in the air carelessly. "Your pain was a fleeting thing, and it's not like you even need a heart. That little sacrifice from you kept me sated for a century, Nyte."

When she came close enough, she reached for him. Scorching, disconcerting heat flared on Nyte's skin, and he teleported to the far side of the room before she could make contact.

"You do not get to touch me," Nyte growled.

Sarnessa turned her face toward him with a predatory glint in her eyes and a shark's smile on her face, displaying her sharp teeth. She cocked her hip, ensuring the pose accentuated her backside before she forced another pout onto her lips. "We're lovers, my beautiful nocturnus. Lovers are meant to take care of each other. Why can't you see that's what you did? But you fled from me and hid yourself away before I could ever explain. Before I could thank you."

How had he not seen through it before? How had he been so naïve, so foolish? From the beginning, Sarnessa had only sought to satisfy her own desires, her own needs. She'd spoken words of praise and caring, had talked as though she would've moved the world for him...but what had she ever done?

She was a black hole, devouring everything that came near, taking, taking, taking, and giving nothing in return.

The bathroom door opened. Nyte snapped his face toward Ember, who stepped out with her dry hair loose around her shoulders and a towel wrapped around her curvy body. She halted abruptly and gasped as her eyes locked on Sarnessa.

Ember's surprised expression was quickly overcome by a glaring scowl. She crossed her arms over her chest. "I'm assuming this is the infamous succubitch?"

Without thought, Nyte turned insubstantial and whisked himself to Ember, reforming with his body between her and Sarnessa, hands to his sides with claws splayed.

The succubus arched a slender brow, and the corner of her mouth rose in a smirk as she chuckled. "See, Nyte? You can't tell me there's nothing between us when you clearly can't stop talking about me, even to lowly mortals."

"Oh, get over yourself," Ember said. He could practically hear her rolling her eyes.

Sarnessa's eyes narrowed at Ember, but her gaze flicked back to Nyte, her beguiling smile returning. "Don't let a single moment destroy what we had. Don't you remember how I made you feel? Don't you remember everything we shared?"

Running the tips of her claws over her breast and down her belly, she slowly sashayed toward him. Her fingers trailed lower and lower toward her cunt, where her exposed inner labia was swollen with lust. She lightly caressed the folds. "I have missed your touch, my Nyte. I have *craved* it. Especially that wicked, wicked tongue. Do you remember the taste of me?"

Her scent strengthened, and Nyte felt the magic in it, felt its warm caress against his skin, felt it subtly trying to push deeper into him. His mind reeled under the silent assault. Another thing he'd failed to notice, failed to consider—Sarnessa was a succubus, and her fragrance was an aphrodisiac. How much of his desire for her had ever been his own?

"Ugh. It's pretty pathetic how desperate you are," Ember said. "You reek of it."

Sarnessa halted with a disgusted scoff. "Would you put this mortal bitch in her place and muzzle her already? Her yipping is distracting."

Ember stepped beside Nyte and jabbed a finger at the demoness. "The only bitch in here is you, and you're acting like you're in heat. I swear, if you drip anything on my floor..."

Nyte put his arm out, barring Ember's way, though he couldn't stop himself from snickering.

Sarnessa's jaw dropped, disbelief in her eyes. "You laugh?"

"You should be thankful I've done nothing more than that. It is well past time for you leave, Sarnessa."

Glowering, she aggressively gestured at Ember. "Surely you haven't been bespelled by this witch." Her black eyes roamed over Nyte, and then she laughed. "You are! She bound you to her. And you thought *I* was cruel for taking your heart? At least I didn't entrap you."

Nyte bared his fangs, one wing spreading wide while the other curled around Ember from behind. "You will not speak of her. I should gouge out your eyes for merely looking upon her."

Sarnessa's pheromones strengthened, growing potent and heady, shedding all pretense of subtlety as they battered his mind and threatened to overcome his senses. Nyte shook his head. The room around him seemed to waver, and a crimson haze crept into the edges of his vision. He staggered, resisting that overwhelming, insidious influence, but the succubus's attack was unrelenting.

The demoness smiled, her gaze holding his as she closed the remaining distance between them and reached out a hand as though to caress his cheek. "My Ny—"

Ember shoved Nyte's arm down, positioned herself in front

of him—directly in Sarnessa's path—and slapped the demoness's hand away. "Back. The fuck. Up."

Sarnessa gasped, her eyes widening, and for an instant, her mask fell away. All that smugness, that sultry self-assurance, vanished, leaving only genuine shock.

Nyte breathed in. Another scent filled his nose, cutting through Sarnessa's, diluting it, overpowering it. Infinitely sweeter, purer, and more alluring. Fresh gardenia, warm vanilla, and something wholly feminine and unique. Ember's scent.

That fragrance forced back some of the blood red cloud encroaching on Nyte's consciousness. Clutching his head between his hands, he turned all his focus toward Ember's fragrance. Toward breaking free of the succubus's charm.

Sarnessa recovered quickly. Her features twisted, becoming vicious, vile, and vindictive—the first time he'd seen the cruelty and selfishness at her core reflected upon her face. She drew her arm back, claws poised to strike.

Nyte gritted his teeth. He pushed himself forward, but it felt as though he were fighting through viscous sludge, his body sluggish, the air itself resisting his movement. He couldn't allow Ember to be harmed, couldn't allow Sarnessa's blow to connect, but he couldn't move fast enough to intervene.

A shooting star hurtled in front of Nyte and Ember. It crashed into the succubus's face with a blue-white flash, emitting a cloud of glittering stardust.

Ember sucked in a sharp breath.

Sarnessa's head jerked back, and she stumbled a couple steps backward with a startled cry. Starling clawed at the succubus's eyes and cheeks with all four hands and kicked at her mouth with both feet while biting down on the demoness's nose. Sparkling silver flecks fell from her tiny, frantic body.

Darkness gathered around Nyte as Sarnessa's hands darted

up to pry the sprite from her face. Starling latched on with claws and teeth, resisting the much larger demon. Finally, the demoness's flesh tore, and she shrieked as the sprite came free.

"Feral fucking vermin!" Sarnessa hurled Starling aside, her lips peeling back to display her fangs. A chunk of her upper nose was missing, oozing black ichor, and dozens of tiny scratches marred her face. Her furious eyes were twin pools of boiling tar.

That hateful gaze jerked to Ember as Starling struck the wall and fell to the floor.

"Starling!" Ember called.

Growling, Sarnessa lunged at the witch, who flinched back.

Nyte roared. The sound was bestial, resonating from the depths of his soul. He swept his wings forward, protectively enveloping Ember in their star-filled night. Sarnessa's claws bit into them. The flickers of pain caused by her blow could not pierce the veil of Nyte's fury.

He wrapped his arms around Ember, tugging her against his chest, and channeled his magic through his wings as he swung them open. A wave of bristling darkness blasted Sarnessa backward. She let out a pained, furious growl as she hit the far wall.

Dozens of shadowy tendrils lashed toward her, blotting out most of the bedroom's light, their tips hardened into solid black blades. A writhing mass of night given shape and instilled with rage.

Sarnessa's form rippled, and she vanished in a cloud of crimson mist that dissipated when Nyte's shadows struck it.

Keeping Ember held firmly against him, he scanned the room with all his senses, seeking any sign of her. The succubus's scent was already fading. Moments dragged by, marked by the thumping of Ember's heart.

Sarnessa had fled. Of course she had; everything she did

was in the service of herself, was for her own survival. She wasn't the sort to risk everything in a head-on fight. No, she preferred to coerce and manipulate her prey. Even a nocturnus's heart wasn't worth her life.

"Is she gone?" Ember asked.

"Yes." As his shadows faded, Nyte turned Ember to face him, raising her chin with a hooked finger. "Are you all right?"

Her eyes met his, steady despite the shakiness of her breaths. She flattened her hands on his chest. "Yeah. But Starling—"

Nyte sensed the infernal pulse behind him just before Ember's eyes rounded. He yanked his witch protectively against him as something hot as lava plunged into his back, tearing through his physical form. Searing fingers clutched his heart, his core, his very essence.

Agony pervaded him. That crushing grip held him paralyzed, sapped his strength, rendered him helpless. He knew his knees would've buckled were his limbs not locked by pain.

"Nyte!" Ember gasped. He'd never seen such horror and worry on her face, had never felt such pure, potent fear coming from her.

Not fear of him, but for him. She feared for his safety, for his wellbeing, for his life, and he wrapped his mind around that, clung to it, as Sarnessa's hand squeezed. The demoness was pulling on his heart, intent on ripping it out.

Nyte growled and resisted that pull with every sliver of willpower he possessed.

"The strength this granted me the first time...it was exhilarating," Sarnessa purred. "I felt like a goddess. And I deserve to feel that way, always and forever."

Ember tried to pull away from Nyte, but he could only hold on to her, keeping her in place, as Sarnessa's claws sank deeper and she pulled harder.

"No," Ember rasped, shaking her head, fighting against Nyte's hold. "No, please no."

Nyte's heart thrummed in the succubus's grasp. He felt its tethers to the rest of his being stretching, straining, beginning to tear.

"Ah, my beautiful Nyte, your heart is brimming with... What is this?" Sarnessa chuckled, the sound dark, seductive, and sickening. "Love? Did my nocturnus learn to *love*? Oh, this will be delicious."

Ember's brows fell, her nostrils flared, and her jaw tightened. Fear still gleamed in her enthralling blue eyes, but fury outshone it now. "I said *no!*"

Her shout swept through the room on a wave of staggering power, a raw, punishing arcane burst that resonated through every mote of Nyte's being.

That power forced Sarnessa back. She cried out, losing her hold on Nyte's heart as her hand tore free.

Nyte gasped and sagged forward. His body and soul quaked at the echoing pain, at the near sundering that had occurred, at the sudden cessation of all that pressure and agony. Ember caught Nyte, steadying him as everything inside him shifted back into place and the burn of Sarnessa's invasive touch eased.

"I'll gladly feast on your heart after I take his, witch," Sarnessa spat.

Straightening, Nyte spun toward her. The succubus lunged at him, eyes alight with fury.

"Don't touch him!" Ember commanded. Again, her voice flooded the room with magic.

It took shape before Nyte, and he saw it glint in the air as it formed a translucent aegis standing as tall as him and twice as wide. A shield of light.

Sarnessa crashed into the barrier. It rippled with golden

sparks, but did not yield to her, halting her advance dead in its tracks. She reeled backward, dazed.

Baring his fangs, Nyte raised a hand, and his shadows burst from the floor beneath Sarnessa, coiling around her body and trapping her in place. Her eyes widened, and the first hint of fear wafted from her.

She immediately softened her expression, replacing all her fury with exaggerated fear and confusion. "Nyte, please..."

He tightened his shadowy grasp upon her, dragging her down onto her knees. "Would you have stayed your hand, had I begged for mercy?"

"This hunger," Sarnessa sobbed. "It clouds my mind and drives me to madness."

"God, you really are the worst." Ember stepped up beside Nyte, settling her hand on his back where Sarnessa had attacked him, his shadowy flesh having already mended itself. Her touch was soft and warm and gentle, so completely different from Sarnessa's from moments before. It was actual caring, actual comfort.

Starling flitted over to the succubus, practically bristling. "I have heard enough of her drivel."

She sped around Sarnessa, moving so fast that she became little more than a streak of blue-white light. Stardust rained in her wake, landing on the floor to create an unmistakable pattern —a binding circle.

The succubus gnashed her fangs and struggled to swipe her claws, but the shadows restraining her ensured she could not harm the sprite. Once the circle was complete, Starling moved to Ember, lighting upon the mortal's shoulder.

"You know what to do, witchling," Starling said.

The barrier of light flickered and vanished. Removing her hand from Nyte, Ember stepped forward. His heart roared in response to her getting closer to the succubus, but there was something in her posture, something in her movement, that kept him in place.

Clad in only a towel, with her hair hanging in shimmering silver waves, she looked gorgeous, majestic, powerful, confident, imposing...and utterly radiant. Her skin was glowing, truly glowing, with its own soft luminescence.

As Ember spoke, he realized she was reciting ancient arcane words, which flowed from her mouth with an almost mystifying musicality.

Sarnessa's eyes darted over the floor as the stardust circle faintly glowed. She fought the shadows holding her with more desperation, but she could not break free of them. "No... No! Stop! Release me!" Her gaze rose to Ember. The fear radiating from her made her voice quaver. "What are you doing, witch?"

Starling folded her arms across her chest and grinned. "Banishing you. Suck on that, succubitch."

With an animalistic snarl, Sarnessa thrashed, but all her fear and rage could not break the bindings. Ember's words wove their magic around and beneath the demoness. Light erupted from the circle, intensifying even as the light she emitted grew.

His Ember had become a flame.

She was exactly the sort of radiance that should've blinded him, the sort that pained him, but he could not look away. Would never look away.

Sarnessa's face contorted with desperation. She opened her mouth and released a piercing, ferocious, impotent scream. The luminescence blossomed around her and enveloped her.

Ember spoke the final word of the spell.

The mass of light collapsed inward on Sarnessa, flaring bright enough to make Nyte turn his face away and slit his eyes.

In an instant, the glare snuffed out. The succubus vanished with it. Only the arcane circle on the floor remained, its glow rapidly diminishing.

Starling zipped up into the air and twirled. "Yes! I have been waiting so long to see that bitch get hers."

Beside Nyte, Ember staggered. He hurriedly banded an arm around her waist, drawing her body against his. She held him tight, though she regained her footing quickly enough.

The luster of her skin faded like the final embers of a fire going out.

He cupped her cheek and guided her face toward his, smoothing his thumb over her skin. "By all the hells, Ember, are you all right?"

She beamed up at him. "Did you see that? Did you see what I did? Holy shit, I have magic!"

And gods, what magic it had been.

He looked at Starling, who remained nearby wearing a grin that seemed much too large for her little face. "You taught her all that? Taught her a banishment spell?"

Somehow, the sprite's grin stretched wider. "Banishment and binding. Sarnessa will be trapped in the Pit of Despair for many, many, *many* years to come, and her meals certainly will not come easy there. But the rest, our witchling did all on her own."

Nyte's chest swelled as he looked back at Ember, his heart nearly bursting with that huge, complex, delightful emotion called love. He knew it was the only thing holding back all the pain and residual fear he should've been experiencing.

He could've lost her forever tonight...and that only reaffirmed what he had to do once their lunar binding was dispelled.

He drew Ember into an embrace, his clawed fingers slipping into her hair. Part of him wanted to hold her like this forever.

Nyte pressed his lips to her forehead. "Ah, my Ember. How brightly you shine for me."

Chapter Twenty-Three

Smiling and closing her eyes, Ember slipped her arms around Nyte. There was a hint of desperation in the way he kissed her, in the way he held her, and it reflected her own inner turmoil after having watched Sarnessa nearly tear out his heart. After seeing the agony that had been in Nyte's eyes.

She wanted nothing more than to melt against him and forget about the rest of the world.

However brief, the encounter with Sarnessa had been draining in every way possible. Adrenaline hummed within Ember, and residual wisps of magic fluttered through her body. Even if part of her was ready for sleep, she knew she wouldn't get any rest for a while. Not until all this calmed down.

Holy fuck. I...I used magic!

Ember had wondered if it was even possible, if summoning Nyte had been a fluke. Starling had been adamant in her belief that Ember could cast the banishing spell on Sarnessa when the time came. Ember hadn't necessarily shared the sprite's confidence.

Yet not only had she cast Starling's spell, she'd blasted the succubus away from Nyte before the demoness could steal his heart for the second time. Sarnessa wasn't going to hurt Nyte again.

Ember's breath caught.

Nyte...

I'm losing him tonight.

She'd known this moment would come, and she had tried to be strong, had tried to keep her sadness at bay. God, even in the shower she'd struggled to hold back her tears. But she couldn't stop them now. They burned as they filled her eyes.

And she'd thought lying in bed with him during these last moments would be enough? That the memories she'd had with him would be enough? In the span of a month, Nyte had become an essential part of her.

She didn't want to let him go.

Ember curled her fingers against his back and looked up at him. "Nyte..."

A concerned crease formed between his eyebrows, and he took her face between his big, warm hands. "What's wrong, Ember? Did she harm you?"

She shook her head as tears spilled down her cheeks, her bottom lip quivering. Her heart felt as though it was breaking, rending her chest wide open even as it caved in on itself. "I don't want to lose you. I thought I'd be able to let you go, but I... I can't."

The smile that upturned his lips was the gentlest she'd ever seen. Shaking his head, he brushed her tears away with his thumbs. "Come, Ember. Let's watch the moon rise."

His shadowy magic flowed over her skin, making it pebble with that whispery touch. When the shadows faded, her towel was gone, replaced by her favorite warm, cozy white pajamas, which were decorated with blue crescent moons and black cats, paired with fuzzy socks.

"Ooo, yes, let's!" Starling flew closer, beaming.

Nyte turned his face toward the sprite, his smile not fading. "Starling, if I wasn't already, I am eternally indebted to you. Thank you, my friend. But the rest of this night..." He returned his gaze to Ember, and it softened. "This night is for myself and my witch."

Ember's throat tightened, and her chest constricted with emotion. It was taking every ounce of her willpower to keep from crumbling into a blubbering mess. She could fall apart...

After he's gone.

Starling flicked her eyes between Nyte and Ember, and her smile stretched. "Of course." She patted one of Nyte's horns. "I shall see you tomorrow."

And then she was gone, leaving behind only her fading stardust.

Nyte bent and whisked Ember off her feet, cradling her against his chest. She'd only had time to slip her arms around his neck when the world blinked out of existence for an instant. They reappeared on the roof of her house, shadows dissipating around them. The cold breeze blew over her.

He sat down, crossing his legs in front of him and settling her upon his lap, keeping his arms securely banded around her. His tail draped over her leg and hooked behind her knee. Then his wings stretched forward and turned inward, folding around her like a blanket.

Ember looked down at them. It was like staring into an endless, starry sky. She trailed her fingers over his wing, tracing paths between the stars. When Nyte was gone, how would she ever look at the night sky without thinking of him?

"There," he said softly.

With her eyes stinging and the pressure in her chest growing more immense, she forced her attention up.

Despite Salem's ambient nighttime glow, she saw the sliver of moon cresting the buildings on the horizon. Her fingers kept moving on his wings absently as, barely breathing, she watched the moon creep higher, its silver light intensifying as it emerged. The minutes that must've passed felt both like an eternity and an instant.

She was waiting, she realized. Waiting for that inevitable change. For that shift, for the magic binding her and Nyte together to break, waiting to feel the sudden disconnect, the sudden emptiness.

Ember stared at the full, round moon, which was bigger and brighter than seemed possible, and she didn't feel any change inside her. All she felt was the beauty of that sight. The beauty of the night.

She looked at her nocturnus. The only beauty she was interested in was that of *her* Nyte.

He was staring up at the moon, but all she could look at was him.

Her heart thumped in her chest, marking the passing seconds, and that tightness inside her only strengthened. Surely she'd feel something. Their tether was broken now, wasn't it? Was he just going to...to vanish without leaving some part of himself behind? Or would he depart, taking her heart with him, leaving an aching hollowness in his wake?

Unable to hold them back any longer, she let her tears fall.

The corner of his mouth quirked up, and his cosmic, violet-blue eyes lowered to meet hers. That smirk faltered. "Ember..."

Drawing her closer, he combed his claws through her hair, trailing their tips soothingly down her back. "There's no need for all these tears. You're not losing me."

Ember's brow furrowed, and she didn't dare let herself hope. Hope was such a terrible thing. "What...do you mean?"

"I've seen so much in my existence. Watched so many events from afar, so many interactions, so many emotions. And for a long while, I didn't understand them. For me, thought existed well before feeling. Feeling...it required *doing*. Partaking. I've learned joy and sorrow, I've felt anger and betrayal, I've clutched at hope and drowned in despair. I've known fondness and camaraderie, and I have been consumed by lust.

"But there was one emotion that always eluded me. One emotion beyond my understanding, seemingly beyond my ability to feel. Sometimes, I've wondered whether it was real at all. And then you summoned me into your bedroom, and I felt...something. Even that first night. The harder I fought it, the more I tried to suppress it, the more insistent that feeling became."

Nyte lifted a hand to her cheek, sweeping back strands of her hair and tucking them behind her ear as he wiped away the fresh tears with his thumb. "And now I know that love is real. I know because I feel it so wholly, so deeply, that it has become a part of my very being. I learned that from you, Ember. Feel it for you."

Ember's eyes flared. Her heart quickened, beating as fast as a hummingbird's wings, fluttering within her chest. "You... love me?"

He smiled wide, fangs gleaming in the night, and his eyes shone brighter. "I do. When I said I was keeping you, I meant it. And since it's not exactly practical to drag you to another plane of existence with me...it seems I must remain here."

Nyte's words echoed again and again in her mind, and she wondered if she'd imagined them. But no, they were real. He'd spoken them.

He loves me. He loves me.

Ember threw her arms around his neck and pressed her mouth to his. She kissed him even as tears spilled down her cheeks. But they were no longer tears of sadness and grief, they were tears of happiness. Because Nyte wasn't leaving her.

Her fingers clutched at his hair as he slanted his mouth over hers, returning the kiss, deepening it. Their lips caressed, their tongues stroked and entwined. Nyte groaned and lowered his hands to her ass, gripping it and pulling her closer until she was completely flush against him, her knees on either side of his waist.

When she finally broke the kiss, breath ragged, she touched her forehead to his, unwilling to pull away. Ember stroked the tips of his pointed ears with her thumbs and she smiled. "I love you, too, Nyte."

A growl rumbled in his chest, and he pulled his head away. There was a new intensity in his eyes, a new solemnity on his face, a hard set to his features that spoke equally of possessiveness and protectiveness. "Know that I will not watch you grow old, Ember. I refuse to lose you to mortality. Refuse to have a mere taste of a life with you."

He leaned back and lifted a hand to his chest. His flesh darkened, becoming a whirling maelstrom of shadow, which he reached into effortlessly. Alarm blared through her.

When he withdrew his hand, silver light shone from within his closed fingers. He turned it palm up and opened his fist. Ember gasped. The orb of light upon it looked like a star that had been plucked from the heavens, pulsing with swirls of blue and violet just like his eyes.

"Nyte, is that your..."

"I will have all of you, Ember. Forever."

She looked up from his heart. Though his features were intense, there was vulnerability in his eyes. Reaching up, she brushed a lock of hair from his forehead before cradling his jaw. "I meant what I said. I am yours to keep."

"Then keep my heart safe for me, for it is now yours." Nyte pressed his heart to Ember's chest. Its light brightened, and she gasped, feeling its heat and its thrumming magic as it eased into her. It moved deeper into her chest, nestling within her heart, becoming one with it. One with her.

She felt it then—all his love for her, blazing and radiant, filling her from within, binding them together. She felt *him*. Every part of her was suddenly more aware of him. His scent was stronger, his warmth greater, the touch of his body against hers all the more stimulating and thrilling. Each beat of her heart was a beat of his own.

They were interwoven. Bound.

Ember covered his hand with her own, locking her eyes with his. "I'll always keep it safe."

With a growl, Nyte caught the back of her head and dragged her mouth to his in a consuming kiss. The touch of their lips, the taste of him, and feel of his claws on her scalp were more electrifying than ever. She moaned, and her eyes fell shut as she kissed him in return, wrapping her arms around his neck and pressing her breasts to his chest.

She needed him. Needed to feel his body, skin to skin, needed to feel his hands gliding over her, needed to feel his cock thrusting inside her. And she needed it now.

Ember felt his shadowy magic surround them, felt reality disappear for that fraction of a second, felt soft, familiar bedding suddenly beneath her now bare skin.

Her thighs parted, allowing Nyte to nestle between them with his body stretched out over her own. As he kissed her, his hand smoothed down her chest, pausing over her heart—over their hearts—before moving to cup her breast. He kneaded it, caressed it, and rolled her nipple until she was squirming and whimpering beneath him.

"My dear, sweet witch," Nyte whispered against her lips, his violet-blue eyes blazing into hers. "My love."

Smiling, Ember brushed her lips over his. "My beautiful, wicked demon." She wrapped her legs around him, smiling when his tail curled around her ankle. "My wish."

Epilogue

Shadows swirled around Nyte as he slowly walked backward. The dark tendrils adjusted the long-stemmed red roses and black candles lining the foyer, while his hands sprinkled crimson, burgundy, and black rose petals on the floor leading deeper inside from the front door.

Ember had undoubtedly known he was plotting something when he'd left the boutique early today, but that was simply unavoidable. The hours he'd taken off were barely proving adequate to obtain and prepare everything; she was likely on her way home right now, and he wasn't quite done.

For this holiday, he was taking the initiative. And everything had to be perfect.

Nyte still wasn't sure if he understood human holidays. They seemed to mean different things to different people, making it difficult to get a true sense of them.

Halloween had been Ember's favorite, and the city had been overrun with excited tourists and costumed pedestrians in the time leading up to the actual day. While her enjoyment of

Halloween had brought him his own joy, it had also been incredibly busy at the boutique, meaning the two of them had had less time to themselves during the long days.

Of course, he'd stolen whatever moments he could to touch and kiss his witch.

Despite her slowly expanding grasp on her own magic and Nyte's heart making her effectively immortal, Ember had insisted on living her life as she had before. At least for now. And he'd been more than happy to live it with her. Dealing directly with the humans who came into her shop every day remained captivating and fulfilling in ways he could never have predicted.

And when they had the occasional difficult customer... Well, his darling employer had expressly forbidden him from throat-ripping and disembowelments, but he'd had the opportunity to feed upon some exceptional fear from time to time.

Thanksgiving had come next. He and Ember had traveled to her hometown, and she'd introduced him to her family. They had been openly friendly and accepting of Nyte, even if they didn't seem to know what to make of him most of the time. Initially, he'd thought the point of the holiday had been gluttony, but by the time they sat to eat at a large, food-laden table, he'd begun to wonder if it was more about togetherness instead.

He'd been forced to question his conclusion again when Ember's brothers had each proceeded to eat several plates of food, gorging themselves thoroughly enough that he'd feared their stomachs would burst.

Of course, the bit of research he'd done on the holiday had revealed another dark historical chapter, the effects of which were still rippling through the world to this day. He'd been unable but to wonder just how much cruelty and brutality humans covered up or ignored to protect themselves from the sins of their ancestors, thus dooming themselves to repeat the same cycles, the same atrocities.

Trying to reconcile what the day presently seemed to be with what it signified historically had been...difficult, and he'd yet to reach a satisfactory understanding.

Christmas had been about decorations, sweets, and gifts. Again, there seemed to be some deeper meaning to the holiday, but so much of the messaging around it was conflicted. Ember had explained that most holidays had been commercialized, that they'd become primarily about spending money on seasonal goods. But when the two of them had exchanged gifts on Christmas morning, all that mattered to him was her radiance, her smiles, her happiness.

Nyte reached up and touched the silver heart-shaped locket dangling from his neck. Inside was small vial of Ember's blood. He smiled. She'd been anxious when he'd opened the gift and had explained that since she couldn't literally gift him her heart, she was giving him her life's blood instead.

He couldn't think of anything sweeter.

They'd spent New Year's Eve at Maggie and Levi's, nibbling on finger foods—none of which contained actual fingers—and playing games such as Pictionary and Charades. The more wine Ember and Maggie had consumed, the more Nyte and Levi had laughed at their antics. Nyte truly enjoyed it when they spent time with the couple. They were the first friends he'd had apart from Starling, and he deeply appreciated how much they cared for Ember.

He hadn't understood the excitement when they'd turned on the television to watch a glowing ball very slowly and anti-climactically fall, with the three humans counting down out loud once the timer hit ten seconds. Zero had come with a chorus of cheers. But his confusion had swiftly evaporated, giving way to a burning heat in his core when Ember threw her arms around him and pulled him down into a sultry kiss before whispering *happy new year* against his mouth.

Now it was Valentine's Day, and he didn't care what it meant to anyone else. To him, it's purpose was clear—love.

He'd spent every day of the last four months loving Ember, and he would spend every day for the rest of eternity loving her. But he intended to make today special. Today would be a celebration not of some historical event, but of his feelings for her.

Nyte dumped the rest of the rose petals on the foyer's floor and directed his shadows to spread them out in the shape of a large heart around him.

Once done, he turned toward the front door and looked over his work. Candles and flowers were everywhere, and in the living room, he'd arranged blankets and pillows on the floor for another movie night, this time with chocolates and champagne instead of popcorn and wine. More flower petals and candles lay scattered around to provide the proper ambience.

He couldn't wait to lay her down there and show her every bit of love and affection she deserved.

Nyte stilled. He could feel Ember drawing near, and it made his very being thrum with anticipation. The lights were already off, but he willed the darkness to deepen.

Ember inserted the key into the lock. The tumbler turned, and she opened the door. Outside, night had fallen, but it couldn't compare to the inky blackness in the house.

She moved to step inside, hesitating when she realized just how dark it was. "Nyte?"

He snapped his fingers, sending out a burst of magic. The candles closest to the entrance flared to life with purple flames. The fire leapt from candle to candle, one by one, leading toward him, the flickering violet glow chasing back the total darkness and revealing a starlight sky in place of the ceiling.

Ember gasped, her eyes following the path of the flames until the area around him was aglow. "Nyte...this is..."

The beautiful smile she gave him filled his chest with wholesome, uplifting warmth, and though it was no longer technically inside him, he felt his heart swell.

Closing the door behind her, she locked it and dropped her purse on the floor. "This is incredibly romantic."

"It's even more romantic over here." He beckoned her with a crooked finger. "Come, my witch."

Slipping off her heels, she followed the path of rose petals. The flowing material of her white skirt fluttered around her legs as she walked. When she drew closer, Nyte held a hand out to her. As soon as her fingers touched his, he took hold and tugged her close.

She laughed as she fell against his chest. Nyte smiled down at her, drawn in, as he ever would be, by her stunning beauty, her radiant smile, and her bright blue eyes. But he was most taken by the love in her gaze as she looked at him.

"So this is why you left early," Ember said.

"And you've no idea how difficult that was to do."

He'd spent most of the day teasing her. Stealing heated glances, sneaking intimate caresses, taunting her with wisps of shadow trailing up her legs and over her pussy, ensuring that his shirt was unbuttoned just a little more than necessary. He'd loved it when her cheeks flushed and her breath quickened while she was speaking to a customer. And he'd reveled in her attempts to hide her desire as he toyed with her clit, thrilling in her struggles to remain composed.

Best of all had been the lustful gazes she'd cast his way.

Ember tapped his nose. "And *you* know exactly how difficult you made it for me while you were there."

Nyte smirked, curling his tail behind her and brushing it up her calf. "I'm not sure I know what you mean, witch."

"Hmm... That's fine, my demon." She pressed a kiss to his chin, then another on his jaw. "I'm more than happy to show you."

Her lips skimmed down the column of his throat, leaving a trail of kisses that made him shiver even as his core heated. His lips stretched into a smile as he tipped his head back to give her better access.

He tensed, hissing through clenched fangs when her blunt teeth sank into the flesh where his neck and shoulder met. A deep ache blossomed low in his belly, and shadows coalesced at his groin, forming his cock. Nyte flexed his fingers, tempted to whisk her away to the blankets, to be inside her now. But he would wait.

"Vixen," he grated as the pleasure-pain radiated through him.

Removing her teeth, Ember let out a soft laugh, and he could feel the curve of her smile against his neck before she kissed where she'd bitten "My sweet demon."

Her lush lips continued their path, following the length of chain to the locket and then down his chest, stopping at his nipple. He groaned as her tongue teased the spiked piercing.

His body stiffened, his cock throbbing insistently. "Ember..."

She caught his other nipple in her mouth and sucked, flicking that maddening tongue against it. He growled as pleasure unfurled inside him. Closing his eyes, he let his head fall back, his fingers twisting into her hair. He could sense her arousal, could smell it on the air.

Releasing his nipple, she continued trailing a searing path of kisses down his abdomen while slowly lowering herself onto her knees, her nails grazing his sides and hips.

"I've been craving your touch all day," she whispered, teasing his flesh with her breath. "Waiting for you to fuck me. But for now..."

Ember caught the base of his cock, and Nyte snarled when her hot, wet mouth closed around the head of his shaft. He tightened his grip on her hair as she sucked.

"*Fuck!*" he bit out through his fangs. Undeniable pleasure gripped him, making his body go taut. Her tongue undulated along the bottom of his shaft. Each lash struck a chord within him, building a song of ecstasy in his core note by delirious note.

Forcing his eyes open, he looked down at his lovely witch. She gazed up at him with beguiling blue eyes, her dark painted lips stretched around his cock.

"Ah, my beautiful love." Nyte chuckled low as he watched her mouth move over his ridges. "That's it. Suck my cock deep. Show me how much you want my cum."

Her wanton hum reverberated through him, making his body quake. His shaft twitched, and Nyte groaned as his essence seeped from its tip, coaxed by his witch's mouth.

He'd wanted this day to be about Ember, wanted to lavish her with praise, pampering, and pleasure, had teased her all morning in anticipation, but she'd already turned it around on him. A few brushes of those lips and he'd been lost. Despite her desire, despite her need, she was giving to him first. Denying herself for his sake.

And his restraint was fraying with each pull of her mouth and pump of her hand.

He snarled, clutching her hair and trying to stop himself from thrusting. "Fuck, witch, your mouth feels so good."

Nyte needed to see her body, needed to see her kneeling naked at his feet, needed to pleasure her as she was pleasuring him. He needed to feel her moans and gasps around his cock.

Shadows billowed from him, creeping over the floor like rolling fog before climbing up her body. As that darkness enveloped her, her clothing disappeared, leaving nothing to shield that tempting skin from his eyes. A tendril of shadow wound up her inner thigh. When it reached her cunt, it found her already dripping.

Her breath hitched.

"I fucking love this pussy," he purred as more of his shadows swept over her, swirling around her breasts, curling around her nipples and constricting, flicking her clit. "You're always so wet for me."

She shivered and whimpered, parting her thighs further for his shadows, her pelvis rocking. When she moaned, Nyte grunted from the vibrations, which made his cock twitch with a pulse of pleasure. Her breath was ragged and hot against his pelvis, and her brows were pinched in pleasure. Nyte sensed the orgasm building inside her, felt her fighting it.

He smiled and caressed her face. "You suck my cock so beautifully."

His shadows thrummed against her clit.

Ember gasped and drew back, letting his cock slip free of her mouth. "Nyte..."

His hand slid to the back of her head and urged her closer. "Keep going, my love. Don't stop until you've drunk from me."

Keeping her eyes on his, she leaned forward and kissed along the side of his shaft, taunting him with those lips. "Do you want my mouth or my pussy, Nyte?"

When she flicked her tongue over the underside of the head and over his slit, collecting his essence, he shuddered, baring his clenched teeth.

"I'll have them both." He pulled her mouth back over his cock, and she took it, sucking enthusiastically. Nyte hissed, that song within him swelling toward a crescendo.

"Good girl. Yes, suck me deep. I can't wait to eat your pretty pussy, to taste your cum on my tongue. To fill that hot cunt with my cock and fuck it hard and raw. But for now..."

His tail grazed up her essence-coated inner thigh until it reached her sex, where the tip nudged her soaking entrance. She moaned as he pushed it inside her. His core clenched at the feel of her tight pussy, and his cock pulsed with the need to be inside her, to feel the embrace of her inner walls.

He pumped his tail deep, in and out, matching the rhythm of the shadows stroking her clit.

Without stopping that delicious glide of her mouth, she whimpered around his cock, spread her thighs wider, and moved upon his tail.

He watched it all. Watched his cock disappearing into and emerging from her mouth, watched her breasts bouncing, watched her curvy, lush body as he pleasured her, watched her lashes drooping and her eyes heating even as their blue darkened.

His Ember, his witch, his soulmate.

Mine.

She came with a muffled cry, her body stiffening and movements disjointed as she fragmented.

The hot, wet pull of her mouth, her moans, the constriction of her cunt around his tail, and the building pressure within his core became too much to withstand. Nyte's hips moved of their own accord as he gripped her hair to keep her in place, exhilarated by the tight suction of her mouth. Feral, guttural sounds rose from his chest and throat. Her sweet, enticing, erotic scent flooded his senses, so potent that he could almost taste her on her his tongue.

His cock swelled, growing thicker, until finally the torturous pleasure within him combusted in a supernova that blinded him with searing white light.

"Ember!" Nyte snarled, his wings snapping out and shuddering as he held his cock deep in her mouth. His body trembled with that explosion. His essence flooded her mouth, and her throat worked around him, swallowing his release.

He groaned, his grip on her hair slackening as he affectionately petted it, his cock still thrumming with the pleasure sweeping through him. "Fuck, you are perfect. So fucking perfect."

Ember withdrew her mouth, leaving him bereft, but she pumped her fist along his length, making him jolt.

His body trembled at the flare of sensation. Ember didn't stop her hand until it had driven him to another climax, coaxing more ropes of cum out of him. They spilled upon her chest and breasts, sparkling in the purple candlelight.

Rapt, Nyte watched his release trickle over her skin, watched as it coated her, as it beaded upon the tip of one of her hard nipples. Something deep and primal rumbled within him.

All. Fucking. Mine.

He caught her chin and caressed her swollen lower lip with his thumb, smearing her lipstick further. "Such a good fucking girl."

Ember smiled and kissed his thumb.

Nyte smirked and slid his tail free of her, enjoying the way she shivered. He raised it to his mouth. Her grip on his cock tightened as she watched.

Without looking away from her, he parted his lips and slipped the tip of his tail between them, sucking off her essence with a growl. "You are delicious."

He willed his shadows to swirl around them like gathering storm clouds. "Now it's my turn."

The darkness swallowed them both, shifting them through space in a tingling rush. When they rematerialized, they were in the living room atop the blankets he'd laid out, with Ember on her back and his mouth on her cunt.

Nyte speared her with his tongue, and her cry filled the room as his shadows lovingly caressed her.

Her hands flew to his horns, gripping them tight as she bore down on him. "Nyte..."

He chuckled against her.

Oh, how he would make his Ember burn.

Author's Note

Thank you all so much for reading! We hope you loved Nyte and Ember's story. We had so much fun writing it and adored all the interactions between the two (and every scene with Starling too).

This project started off with Opal coming to us with a simple prompt: *a witch accidentally summons a monster, and make it fun and spicy!* It was a blast seeing what all of us came up with, and how different our stories were. We hope you guys enjoy each and every one!

Please consider leaving us a review, and we'd be ever so grateful if you could recommend us to a friend or share our books on your socials. Word of mouth is the best way you can help support an author.

To stay up to date with what we're working on, our progress, and any other updates we might have, be sure to join our newsletter! Don't worry, we don't spam. We send out a monthly newsletter on the first of each month, and a few others here and there if we have a sale or something to announce. We also have a reader group on Facebook if you'd like to join that as well.

Again, thank you all! We can't thank you enough for your support.

Also by Tiffany Roberts

THE INFINITE CITY

Entwined Fates

Silent Lucidity

Shielded Heart

Vengeful Heart

Untamed Hunger

Savage Desire

Tethered Souls

THE KRAKEN

Treasure of the Abyss

Jewel of the Sea

Hunter of the Tide

Heart of the Deep

Rising from the Depths

Fallen from the Stars

Lover from the Waves

THE SPIDER'S MATE TRILOGY

Ensnared

Enthralled

Bound

THE VRIX

The Weaver

The Delver

The Hunter

THE CURSED ONES

His Darkest Craving

His Darkest Desire

ALIENS AMONG US

Taken by the Alien Next Door

Stalked by the Alien Assassin

Claimed by the Alien Bodyguard

Saved by the Alien Crime Boss

STANDALONE TITLES

Claimed by an Alien Warrior

Dustwalker

Escaping Wonderland

Yearning For Her

The Warlock's Kiss

Ice Bound: Short Story

ISLE OF THE FORGOTTEN

Make Me Burn

Make Me Hunger

Make Me Whole

Make Me Yours

VALOS OF SONHADRA COLLABORATION

Tiffany Roberts - Undying

Tiffany Roberts - Unleashed

VENYS NEEDS MEN COLLABORATION

Tiffany Roberts - To Tame a Dragon

Tiffany Roberts – To Love a Dragon

WITCHES LOVE MONSTERS COLLABORATION

Oops! I Summoned a Night Demon

About the Author

Tiffany Roberts is the pseudonym for Tiffany and Robert, a husband and wife author duo. The two have always shared a passion for reading and writing, and it was their dream to combine their mighty powers to create the sorts of books they want to read. They write character driven sci-fi and fantasy romance, creating happily-ever-afters for the alien and unknown.

Sign up for our Newsletter!
Check out our social media sites and more!
http://www.authortiffanyroberts.com

www.ingramcontent.com/pod-product-compliance
Ingram Content Group UK Ltd.
Pitfield, Milton Keynes, MK11 3LW, UK
UKHW041951230426
12048UKWH00008B/268